# Darkness

# in Durrington

Written by Derek McMillan

Edited by Angela McMillan

This edition published by Amazon 2019

All characters fictitious

# Dark Satanic Mills

Chris Mills was a nasty little man. His pupils used to call him "Dark Satanic Mills". So did the other teachers. It was hardly surprising therefore that his body was found in a skip. Even Micah thought he "probably asked for it."

The first I knew about his demise was when Micah positively snorted over an obituary in the *Worthing Herald.*

"Listen to this, Craig. The idiot clearly didn't know Chris Mills. He was fair in hair colour and in nothing else. He was the nastiest person I have ever met and I've met murderers and drug dealers in this job."

"So you're not a fan?"

This asinine question earned me another snort.

"Listen to this, 'Pupils and staff of the Stinger School in Westington are mourning the loss of a much-loved and respected member of staff. Chris Mills was a well-known local figure and the life and soul of the Maths Department.'"

"Well that's the first I've heard of the Maths Department having a soul but if it was Mills then it really was condemned for eternity," she added.

"That's rather uncharitable."

"You never met him."

Micah continued reading, "'The body of the 35-year-old was found in a skip in New Road, Durrington on Tuesday morning. Mr Mills had been strangled. The police are appealing for witnesses."

"Best thing that could have happened to him," Micah concluded.

The conversation took place in the John Selden. The bar was an excellent place for us to hold business meetings. Not only was there food and wine available, there were often clients, potential clients and the odd time-waster. Even time-wasters could be expected to buy their round and often provided colourful if irrelevant stories.

Speaking of which, Gerry had joined us.

"It is a mistake to wish your enemies dead, Micah," he started. "You know Lenin's elder brother, Aleksandr Ulyanov, was a Narodnik. The high point of the achievements of the Narodniks was to assassinate the Czar. All that achieved was that there was another Czar to take his place and by all accounts he was even worse than the one before."

If any readers can make head or tail of this story in the context of the death of Mr Mills, please let us know.

Gerry went on to say, "You realise that finding out who killed Dark Satanic Mills would be a feather in your cap, don't you."

"I am more interested in pennies in the bank account than feathers in caps," said Micah somewhat tartly.

We went on to talk of other matters but the issue came back to haunt us when I received a telephone call three days later.

"You don't know me, Mr McLairy, but my name is Ellen Price née Ellen Mills. It is my brother whose body was found in a skip. I know who killed him. I told the police but they paid me no attention. The short and long of it is that I've had mental health problems in the past so they think that invalidates my evidence."

"How can I help you?" I asked with the state of the bank balance in mind, rather than any certainty that she knew the murderer's identity.

"Mr McLairy, I know about you. I know the Durrington Detective Agency can work miracles when the police are stymied. I want to make an appointment. I won't go to the John Selden, I would like to come to your office and make a statement. After that, if you think I have a case, I want you to bring the culprit to justice."

We arranged to meet the following day. I had Micah with me. I do not like to talk to strange women without a chaperone.

Our so-called office was a spare room about the size of a cupboard. In it were my old desktop on the top of an even older desk, Micah's sleek new laptop and three chairs.

Mrs Price was in her early forties but just beginning to go grey. She was dressed very smartly for the occasion in a blue trouser suit. She had a look of Theresa May about her but I pushed that unpleasant thought aside and greeted her amicably.

"It was Graham Noyce," she said without any preamble. "He was a student who absolutely hated our Chris when he was at school and only waited to attack him until he had left and couldn't be punished by the school."

I didn't like to say that hating Mr Mills was hardly unusual and that schools do not normally punish murder with detention or lines.

"What evidence do we have?" Micah asked.

"That's your department, isn't it? I want you to find the evidence and get the little tyke put behind bars. I will pay your usual rate plus expenses."

"We will do as you ask, Mrs Price..."

"Ms"

"Ms Price. However you realise that the facts might point to a different culprit."

"They won't."

"...in which case we will have to present our findings to the police."

"I quite understand but it was Graham Noyce spelt N o y c e. Make no mistake."

As we were making our way to New Road, the scene of the skip, I asked Micah if she had any personal reasons for disliking Mills.

"It wasn't personal. It was the type of teacher he was. Some teachers like to lord it over their pupils because, unsurprisingly, they know more than they do. Others like to encourage whatever talent the pupil has, even if the evidence may take some digging to find. We disliked each other on principle. And he wasn't a union member."

"That's the sin against the Holy Ghost," I said.

"Not helpful, Craig."

The owner of the skip wasn't helpful either.

"I dunno."

"When did you find the body in your skip?"

"I didn't. It was some passer-by who spotted it on Tuesday morning. I was still in bed."

"Have you any idea..."

"No."

"I haven't asked the question yet."

"I'm sorry, mate, I just have no idea. They gave me another skip though so everything's OK."

"Except for the dead man."

"Well he ain't worried is he?"

The man, a Mr Prendergast, laughed like a drain at his own joke and we left him to it.

"Micah," I said.

"We need to find out the identity of the passer-by. I'll get on it as soon as we get home. I will also..." and she went off into a contemplative silence.

I started cooking the sausages and fried onions while Micah used her dark arts on the laptop. The police system is secure but there is one officer (who can now be named as old Ben Tillotson) who downloads confidential files to a laptop which Micah can easily access. She misses the challenge of hacking closed systems sometimes but it has made our work a lot easier.

She came back with an old fashioned notebook full of information.

"Death was due to strangulation. Conventional wisdom is that the perpetrator has to be heavier or taller than the victim. More often than not the killer is male. However that does not apply in this case because he was strangled with a twisted rope. A child of five could have done it. We have no five-year-old on the list of suspects."

"The body was found by Chas Chalmers who was on his way to Durrington Tesco but was distracted by the 'dead geezer in the skip.' He apparently knew Mills as he called it 'good riddance to bad rubbish'. This made him suspect number one."

"However the death occurred within a 'window' of 2 to 3 am and several witnesses can verify that Chas Chalmers was drunk and incapable in Pond Lane recreation ground at that time. It would seem he was off to Tesco so early to get some cider."

"I still think we can interview Chas Chalmers for the local press (Micah did once write an article for the *Worthing Journal* which they didn't publish. She is therefore a very free freelance) and we could offer our condolences to Mrs Mills."

"I have the addresses. Let's get on."

Chas Chalmers had the sort of concentration span that a night of drinking and a day consuming two quarts of Strongbow induces.

He was clear on one thing though, "There'll be some money in it for me, then," he said.

I think he had morning breath 24/7 and it was all I could do to nod while holding my breath. This could go one of two ways. He could remain silent until the cash was in his hands (the wise course). He could blabber away without a firm financial commitment (the foolish course).

Chas turned out to be a foolish blabberer which was to our advantage.

"There was this blue twisted rope round the neck of this geezer in the old skip and you can believe me or not but I swear that his face was much the same colour so I didn't recognise him right off."

"Then I got over (and here he gave a prodigious burp) … Better out than in. I got over the wassisname."

"Shock?" Micah suggested, making notes in her notebook.

"Yeah. When I got a good look at his face and ignored how blue it had got, I clocked it was old Dark Satanic Mills but he certainly weren't alive with the sound of music."

We chose to ignore the mixed musical message. Chas laughed, then he wheezed and started to cough. The coughing went on until he had lit a cigarette.

"One funny thing though. His clothes were all front to back. They do say," he lowered his voice, "those who meet the devil on the road would end up like that. Mills has gone where he deserved to go."

"Singularly unobservant young man," Micah said as we made our way to Mrs Mills' house, "I got the PM results this morning and they make interesting reading. Mills had had a lethal cocktail of alcohol and Phencyclidine which could easily have finished him off. It is likely that the PCP was in his drink because there were no traces in the lungs so it was not inhaled or smoked. The murderer or murderers wanted to make assurance doubly sure. He would have been unable to resist as the rope choked the life out of him."

"And the back-to-front clothes?" I said because I guessed she wanted me to ask.

"I'm glad you asked that. After death, I repeat **after**, the head was twisted round like something out of The Exorcist. The clothes were not back to front as our young friend would have realised if he had observed the hands and feet."

"So do we still think a five-year-old could have done it?"

"The point about the injury being post-mortem is that it would not require strength. It would only require time."

Grace Mills recognised Micah straight away.

"Micah! It was good of you to come. This must be Craig. Do come in, I'll make some tea. No don't stand there looking mournful, come on in."

She wasn't a picture of grief but she explained this to us.

"You met Chris, Micah, you knew what he was like."

Micah made sympathetic noises. She is good at that.

"Well you didn't know the half of it. He was sober at work. After a drink or two the devil got into him. I tell you, Micah. I'm glad we had no kids so they didn't have to witness what that swine...but I shouldn't speak ill of the dead."

Micah patted her hand and searched around for another topic.

"Are you still working in Costa in Durrington Tesco's?"

"Yes. We haven't seen you in there for a while."

I tuned out of this chat and looked at the room. Everything was neat and tidy in a retro style. The furniture was old but well-maintained. The carpet was canary yellow which is not to everyone's taste. The walls were surprisingly bare. No pictures of family, no pictures at all. The telephone was an old Bakelite model which looked as if it were an original. There were no books.

I tuned back in just in time to hear an almost-whispered reference to "forcing his attentions on me" from Mrs Mills.

I claimed a call of nature which took me upstairs and I was able to search all the rooms while Micah kept Mrs Mills chatting about the old days when Grace had been a dinner lady at the school and Micah had been an English teacher.

My search threw up nothing out of the ordinary. The same austere but tidy theme was continued upstairs with a sixties throwback bathroom for good measure.

Our next port of call was, of course, noted local drug dealer, Graham Noyce. Micah reprised her role as a local journalist. This time she was seeking background colour on the deceased for a possible follow-up article.

Micah may be, indeed she is, a doyenne of the modern world of computers, mobile devices and something called "apps". However, I pride myself that I can search a dustbin like a professional. I could list the contents of Noyce's shared dustbin and give various insights into his diet but I will spare the reader this.

Two separate items took my interest. One was an old wallet and the other, even further down the failed lasagne, damp stale bread and tea bag heap, was a Costa card for Mr Christopher Mills. I left them where they were after photographing them. I thought some young DC might like to hone his bin-searching skills on them some time soon.

"Something stinks about this."

"Sorry, Micah."

"I mean apart from you, obviously, Craig. I mean Noyce is young in years but old in villainy. Would he take the wallet from a man he had recently killed and leave it in the communal dustbin of the house he was living in? There are plenty of other dustbins in Durrington which would not point to him as the culprit. It points to his innocence rather than his guilt."

"What did he have to say for himself?"

For answer, Micah turned on her mobile phone. She has the habit of recording her conversations for future reference.

"I knew the old swine but I don't think the local newspapers want to publish anything I want to say."

"Why would that be?" asked Micah.

"Well a lot of it would be four-letter stuff. He was the worst bully I ever came across and I came across enough in the playground, believe me. I know for a fact the other teachers thought he was a bit much. He weren't the life and soul of anything I can promise you. He was more the death and erm whatever the opposite of soul is."

"Spiritual vacuum?" Micah offered.

"Ha ha. Very good. You never taught me but I remember you were an English teacher. A reporter now then. That must be a come down."

"Going back to Mr Mills."

"Dark Satanic Mills, you mean."

"Well going back to him for a minute, when was the last time you saw him?"

"When I left school. About a year ago that was."

"What have you been doing since?"

"Oh a bit of this and a bit of that. Keeping my hands busy, Mrs McLairy."

A small matter of three convictions for drug dealing is not the sort of thing to discuss on the doorstep.

We discussed the case over an Italian beef casserole and a bottle of Chianti that evening.

"Graham Noyce has no alibi for the time of the murder," Micah began, referring to her notes or probably Ben Tillotson's notes from his laptop.

"That cuts both ways. I can't imagine him committing a murder without an alibi or two in hand," I suggested.

"Well I think you will have to keep an eye on young Mr Noyce," Micah said, "He hasn't seen you before so it should be easy enough to tail him. What other suspects do we have?"

Micah turned her notebook to another page. At the top she wrote "random mugger" without a great deal of conviction.

Graham Noyce

Any other pupil with a grudge

Ditto parent

Mrs Mills

"That's just for completeness. The wife is always number one suspect with lover in close second place. I don't think Grace Mills has it in her. She obviously doesn't miss Chris a great deal and I can sympathise with her," Micah said.

"The house is one where no money has been spent for a long time but a lot of effort has been put in to make it into a home. I think we could leave Grace Mills on the list. What would bother me is the fact that she didn't seem remotely nervous. Even if she ended up killing him, something was keeping her from feeling apprehensive that she would go to jail for it." I said.

The next day it was my task to watch the house which Noyce shared with a couple of other lads of about the same age. I was up early but that was a triumph of hope over experience. Noyce didn't stir from the place all day. Another youth left the premises at about opening time. I thought he might have some useful information and as I surmised he headed for the local hostelry. I wasn't averse to a drink myself by this stage in the day.

Young Jimmy Taylor had a pint by the time I arrived and he was holding forth to anyone who would listen.

"You know when I went out to Afghanistan to join the regiment as a subaltern, the colonel wanted to welcome me and he offered me a cigar and I said, 'No, sir, I don't smoke.' He offered me a very fine brandy but I said, 'No, sir I don't drink.'"

That got a few laughs I can tell you, but Jimmy ploughed on, raising his voice he added,

"And then he asked me if I ate hay. When I denied it he said, 'you're not fit company for man or beast.'"

I was to find out that Jimmy had many stories but this was the only one I am prepared to repeat partly because they got progressively coarser and partly because I believe the tale dates back to Kipling's time.

I joined in the general laugh and Jimmy introduced himself and indicated that he would not be averse to me buying him a drink. I introduced myself as John, a time-honoured name shared by Watson.

After a couple of drinks I was his "best mate in the whole wassisname." He told me his opinion on everything and I thought he would get around to talking about his fellow-residents at some point. I was not disappointed.

The door opened. Noyce walked in.

"Well look who it isn't. Jeremy Clarkson," Jimmy Taylor said in a voice which could be heard in Goring.

Noyce did not look pleased and made a gesture to Jimmy to stay away. Jimmy stayed away. He even lowered his voice.

"Watch wass he does."

"Why do you call him Jeremy Clarkson?" I asked.

"We all calls him that 'ere. Issa joke. The legendary presenter of Top Gear."

I watched, I thought subtly, as Noyce went to three targeted customers and spoke to them briefly. He ostentatiously took a cigarette out of a packet and headed for the door.

"As I tell you what. I tell you what. I tell you what."

I was beginning to wonder what Jimmy was going to tell me, if anything, when he went on, "The barman dusnold with old Jeremy Clarkson 'andin over his top gear in the bar so 'e's off to the car park. Mark my words, though, mark my words. The landlord'll 'appily take 'is money over the bar. That's why 'e's never been barred you see. Never been barred."

I saw the three customers casually make their way out of the bar and back in again to be followed by Noyce.

Noyce recognised Jimmy now and came over. He was a handsome expensively-dressed teenager with a ready smile.

He had a hand full of money and bought drinks for Jimmy, for me because I was talking to Jimmy, for the barman and for a bloke who had been standing by the bar getting steadily more disreputable and laughing like a hyena at Jimmy's stories. He didn't count the change although he had been blatantly overcharged.

"So, Jimmy's mate, what do you do for a living?"

I decided I sold cars. This was a mistake because we spent the rest of the evening discussing Noyce's next purchase which was likely to be an Audi which regrettably was not in my range.

At closing time, I dawdled behind and wished them goodnight, saying I wanted a word with the barman. The barman clearly did not want a word with me but he was too polite to say so.

We chatted amiably about the customers. He declared that the man he called "Jeremy Clarkson" was "a character". On the off chance, I showed him a photo of Chris Miles.

"Oh he's been in a few times. He usually has a little chat with old Jeremy about "top gear" if you know what I mean."

I knew what he meant and it was going to cost him his licence when I passed this on to Inspector Ben Tillotson. Deporting the drug-dealing side of the business to the car park was not going to save him when he was clearly taking money off the dealer.

I went home to Barker. Micah was already asleep. I made a few notes for the morning and counted it a good day's work.

For the next few days I dogged Noyce's footsteps. Sometimes I had Barker. Sometimes I was alone. Always I was discreet and I could swear Noyce did not realise he was being followed. However it was all in vain because his footsteps only went to the pub and back.

Micah had more luck because she had an ability to, I think the term is "hack into" telephones which could have got her a job on the *News of the World* in the old days. She had a list of the numbers Noyce had rung in that period and one of them leapt out at us.

"Why was he ringing that number?" Micah asked. It was a rhetorical question but a very interesting one for all that.

We discovered that the police had systematically questioned the staff at the school but they had a staff training course which provided an alibi of sorts. The course was in Chichester and it was highly unlikely that any of them could have returned to Durrington in time to commit the murder.

"Well it's the first time a staff training course has been of any use to anybody," Micah said.

They had the opposite problem with the disgruntled pupils and ex-pupils. There were simply too many of them and none that could be described as "gruntled". The long slow business of sorting out the whereabouts of over two thousand teenagers was continuing.

"And it might have been any one of them," Micah said, "If it were not for that phone call."

I nodded.

Micah was christened Christine. She adopted the name Micah as an act of teenage rebellion. She might not have been a prophet but she certainly had powers beyond the human when it came to the internet.

Armed with the name of the person Noyce had phoned, she soon had an address, the estimated value of the property, the make and number of a car, a National Insurance number, date of birth and highly confidential bank account details.

She did not have access to the CCTV at Noyce's local because that was not connected to the internet. That information was my department.

I met the landlord out of working hours and he was as unwelcoming as a basically polite man can be. I didn't tell him I was with the police but then again I didn't tell him that I wasn't.

"I need to see the CCTV footage for Tuesday night."

"Why is that, John?"

"We have reason to believe there have been illegal drug dealings in the car park and some of the people in this bar might have been involved. You will appreciate we need to keep this between ourselves. I really don't want the licensing authorities to get to hear of it."

"Well that has nothing to do with me."

"Then I expect you will want to co-operate."

His indecision was written all over his face but eventually he nodded and I had a chance to examine the grainy CCTV images.

It would have been too much to hope that Noyce had been dealing drugs in plain view of the cameras but I did notice two interesting encounters.

The bar camera showed that Noyce had been his usual expansive self that evening and treated everyone to drinks. "Everyone" in this instance included Chris Mills. Noyce escorted him to the car park. Mills was already having a job putting one foot in front of another but that was not unusual from everything we knew of the man and his habits. Noyce returned alone. He made no attempt to conceal the cash he had suddenly acquired. Indeed he seemed quite satisfied with it.

The other thing I noticed was a white Peugeot 107 leaving the car park. The number matched the one I had written down from Micah's notes. There were clearly two people in the car but I could not identify them. I didn't need to. If Mills was in the car he was snugly curled up in the boot.

We had a business meeting with Inspector Tillotson in the John Selden that evening. As usual I was buying, which he thought was right and proper.

"What have you got?" he asked, wiping his mouth and putting down a half-full glass of Harveys.

We showed him the CCTV footage on my phone with the sound off and identified the main characters.

"Noyce is well known to us of course. From what you tell us about his habits we can nab him on the way to the pub. We were waiting until we could get a line on his supplier but now there is the small matter of murder to consider."

"And I have a little something for you."

Micah bridled at his use of a conjunction to start a sentence but we listened anyway. They had been researching the provenance of the blue rope and it turned out to be an anti-climax. Mr Prendergast eventually remembered he had left some very similar rope in the skip so it was likely the murderer (we silently amended that to murderers) had picked it up on the spur of the moment.

"It would have been clear that Mills was not long for this world with that lethal combination of drugs and alcohol. Circumstantial evidence from the CCTV puts Noyce firmly in the frame for that."

We made a few arrangements with old Ben and he seemed satisfied with the meeting.

On the following evening we had a meeting with our client. We told her we had some good news. Micah gave her an itemised account and we insisted on cash.

Ellen Price was as neatly turned-out as before and had the money ready in her capacious handbag.

"You'll be pleased to know that Graham Noyce was picked up by the police earlier this evening. He was en route to the pub. He was in possession of enough drugs to prove intent to supply. CCTV coverage from the pub can be used to verify that the PCP came from him so he will be charged with murder."

I paused to let Ms Price enjoy her moment of triumph before adding the word, "However."

She looked up.

"Your car was seen leaving the car park. Both you and your sister-in-law, Mrs Mills, were in that car. You see we have to account for the unnecessary strangulation and the breaking of Mr Mills' neck. Also the way the corpse was moved the best part of a mile from the pub car park."

She was silent for a moment before shouting "THAT BASTARD".

Calming herself, she continued, "I'll tell you about my brother. What kind of man uses PCP on his own wife? You know it is a date rape drug but it also causes horrific hallucinations. Grace thought she was going mad until she learnt the truth."

"She learnt the truth?"

"From me of course. Brother or no, he was a child of Satan."

"There are two police officers in our front room, Ellen." I could see she was considering making a run for it.

"They will take you in. Other officers are going to pick up Grace. You must tell the police as much of the truth as you know. Your brother's behaviour may be seen as provocation and it will certainly be taken into account by the court."

I handed her over to the police. She went quietly.

"One thing bothers me," Micah said, "why on earth did she point the finger at Noyce after he'd worked with them to kill Mills?"

I murmured, "the symbol of Alsace Lorraine."

Micah smiled, "I see. The double cross. So she planted the wallet in the bin. We don't know what he rang her about but it is a bit of luck he did. She hoped Noyce would go to prison and they would walk free."

"It was a forlorn hope. Noyce would grass on his own mother if he needed to. They will get a higher sentence for conspiracy to murder now."

And so it proved. All three were busy accusing each other in court but the outline of the conspiracy was enough to earn them long custodial sentences.

"But he deserved to die," Micah objected.

"That doesn't mean people can take the law into their own hands. Nor can they begin sentences with 'But'."

We drove from the court to the John Selden for dinner. This time old Ben was paying.

# How it all began

So many people ask me how the Durrington Detective Agency began that I think it is about time to tell that story. I was invalided out of the army after an unfortunate difference of opinion with a night club bouncer left me unfit for active service. I returned to teaching where I found I was in the room next to a Christine Backhouse who taught English and a new subject called Information Technology.

She spent her breaks doing something arcane with the computers.

"A teacher cannot be expected to function without coffee," I mentioned from the doorway of her room.

Silence. I repeated the observation.

"Oh I see, Craig, could you possibly get me a mug of coffee? I have to finish this program." She smiled.

The screen was full of incomprehensible code. When I returned with the coffee, she attempted to explain it to me. I tried to look as if I understood a word she was saying.

"You didn't understand that, did you?" she said.

"Not really," I admitted.

"Well, have a look at this." She handed me a book called *Basic for Dummies.*

"Thank you, Christine."

"My friends call me Micah."

She smiled again.

Later I plucked up courage and I invited her for a drink after work in the John Selden.

When Micah arrived I could see she was excited but I didn't imagine the prospect of a drink with me was bringing a shine to her eyes. I was right.

"What are you doing in the holidays?" she asked.

"I may go away for a few days but I have no definite plans. How about you?"

"I have a job. One that's going to make me 500 pounds if I do it right and nothing if I do it wrong. You know Charlie Tillotson?"

"I know his father is the sort of police officer who gives bigots a bad name."

"That's the one. His mother, Else, who I have seen at parents' evenings, has been threatened and she wants me to investigate."

"Why did she call on you, when her husband is in the police?"

"That is because Ben's computer skills are in their infancy and not likely to get their milk teeth any time soon. He is as mad as a hornet about her giving the job and five hundred of his well-earned quid to a left-footer (his words) but he knows when he is out of his depth."

"Why? Who is threatening Else?"

"Her computer."

Well that had me hooked. I was three pages in to "Basic for Dummies" but I thought the concept was more Science Fiction than reality. I have always liked Science Fiction. We agreed to meet the next day after mass. We both attended the same church but we went to different services. That was one thing which was to change.

When I entered Micah's room I was met by shelf after shelf of magazines.

"I get the IPUG magazine every month and read it from cover to cover."

"Dog lover?"

"Independent PET User Group. And the PET is..."

She indicated the computer which sat on the table. The Personal Electronic Transactor was one of the earliest of the micro-computers made by Commodore. When in use it had a dark green screen with light green lettering. She turned it on.

Instead of the message showing the computer was ready to use, the screen remained blank. Then one green letter after another appeared on the screen as if they were being typed slowly by an unseen hand.

"I CAN CONTROL YOUR COMPUTER."

This faded and was replaced slowly with:

"I CAN READ YOUR THOUGHTS."

And finally:

"I CAN CONTROL YOUR MIND."

Then this faded and the sinister trio of messages repeated themselves.

We were quiet for a moment.

"Do you fancy a cup of tea?"

I did.

This was back in the dark ages. The internet was just a twinkle in a programmer's eye in those days so the problem was in the PET itself.

Micah gestured to a pile of ordinary cassette tapes on the table.

"Those are the programs. I want to test them out on my computer but I wonder if you could do me an enormous favour?"

I was keen to get in Micah's good books so an 'enormous favour' seemed a good idea. I nodded.

"Could you go round and have a chat with Else? Reassure her but see what you can find out. Can you do a verbatim report on the discussion?"

"I can with the aid of a tape recorder," I said.

Young Charlie opened the door. Ben was at work but Else was in no state for conversation. She was lying on the kitchen floor with a broken cup and the contents strewn around her and she was SCREAMING.

I got Charlie to phone for an ambulance and sat on the floor with Else. I had a go at holding her hand but she tried to crush my fingers so I gave that up as a bad job,

"Tell me about it?" I asked.

"THE CEILING! THE CEILING! THE CEILING!"

I knew what this was but I couldn't believe it. She thought the ceiling was coming down to crush her like a heroine in a Hammer Horror film. The difference was that in her mind there was no escape, no hero coming to rescue her. I only knew of one thing which could cause this and the medics, when they arrived, confirmed it. Else had taken a near-fatal dose of LSD.

While Else went to hospital, Charlie and I waited in the kitchen for old Ben to arrive. I noticed the back door, which led on to the kitchen, was unlocked. Charlie confirmed that this was always the case with people in Durrington. It was in those days. If someone was in the house, the back door was unlocked.

When old Ben came home, he took charge. The kitchen was a crime scene and Charlie and I were ordered out. Then he didn't know what to do. He should be there for the forensic team when they arrived but he wanted to be in the hospital with Else.

"Mr McLairy. I am leaving you in charge. You are not to go into the kitchen. Just keep an eye on Charlie in the living room and show the forensic team to the kitchen when they arrive."

"Certainly."

"Just repeat the instructions."

And I did.

Charlie was uncomfortable having a teacher in the house but he was a lot happier when I put the TV on.

"I'm hungry, Mr McLairy."

"Well you know we can't go in the kitchen and I can't pop out to get food. I'll phone for a Chinese if you like."

He did like. By the time the Chinese arrived (far too much food for one meal, I always over-order) the forensic team had taken me to the station for fingerprinting and a statement. Charlie had to eat it all himself. He didn't complain.

I mentioned that I didn't want Charlie left alone.

"We'll take care of that, Mr McLairy," said one officer. I remembered him as a pupil and I imagine ordering me about was payback for him.

I wrote the statement longhand which seemed time-consuming. The tape recorder was taken from me although it contained no evidence. They gave me a receipt and I did eventually get it back.

"You will have to take out that bit about LSD, McLairy," the officer said.

"Why?"

"You're not an expert. The statement from the medics is admissible. Your statement isn't. Just write about what you saw. And is that your best handwriting?"

"I'll make it as neat as I can, officer."

"See that you do."

I overheard a conversation in the corridor outside.

"Ben's wife would never have taken LSD. Someone must have gotten in. We have taken the tea caddy and the milk and everything she might have had a nibble of for tests. We will find it there."

"What about the threats she was getting?"

"From her computer? Be your age."

I went back home and met up with Micah in The Lamb in Durrington Lane. There were no wide-screen TVs in pubs in those days. Most pubs were civilised places to take a girlfriend.

"Any luck with the computer?" I asked.

"There is nothing odd about the programs. I was only testing them for thoroughness. It must be the PET. The only company in the area which handles PET computers is Computawares. They came into the money when West Sussex County Council decided to make the PET their standard school computer. In addition to sales they run a very lucrative sideline in repairs. The PET needs a lot of repair work."

The PET was a clumsy lump of metal to manoeuvre so I offered to give Micah a lift and carry the beast for her.

"I can carry a computer, Craig," she said, then she looked at me. I must have looked disappointed.

"And it's a very kind offer which I will take you up on," she added.

The next day we took the PET to Computawares. The premises were in Montague Street up a flight of rickety stairs and judging by the plethora of hardware in the workroom, it was sorely in need of expansion.

A man whose badge said he was the general manager, Anton Debrey, greeted us.

"Look we've got a bit of a backlog," he gestured to the workbench and the sick and dying computers on it, "so it will be at least a month until..."

"This PET is most unusual," said Micah, quietly.

"What, does it do tricks?" he laughed at his own joke.

"Only the one trick. And we have brought it a long way."

We hadn't brought it a long way but I was to learn that Micah would sacrifice the truth if it meant getting closer to the facts.

"All right, show us, darling. I'm only doing this for you."

Micah clearly disapproved of being patronised but needed his help.

I heaved the PET onto a spare space on the workbench and we found a spare plug to connect it to.

The screen glowed green and repeated its bizarre message.

Anton's face went a funny colour as he watched.

He switched to a businesslike mode with admirable speed, "Well it's the 6502 chip. I'm afraid it will need replacing and I'm sorry, darling, but it's going to cost you a pretty penny."

As he was doing the work and Micah was counting out the money, she asked sweetly, "Any idea what caused it to do that?"

She was watching Anton closely.

"Oh, I dunno. Some joker at the factory, perhaps."

"Yes of course. So the fact that the owner was poisoned yesterday would probably just be a coincidence," Micah said.

Anton dropped his soldering iron but again he recovered himself and carried on with the job as if nothing had happened.

Micah took the rogue chip with her in a plastic bag and we made our way carefully down the stairs.

We heard raised voices, or one raised voice and one less raised trying to placate the shouter.

"You can't stop flirting, can you?"

That was all we caught before the conversation quietened down. Micah was all for staying to hear more. I was trying to balance the PET on the staircase and anyway in those days I was not up for eavesdropping.

We adjourned to the Hare and Hounds. I didn't go there often because, despite the name, they don't have dogs or hare for that matter. However since my dog Wolf (he was an Alsatian like Barker) died I thought I would give it another go. The food and wine were as excellent as I remembered.

"He had a guilty conscience about something," I suggested.

Micah was silent and I wondered if she had heard. Then she said, "He might have just been clumsy and a bit surprised. I know Anton of old. I have had a number of computers repaired by him and he always flirts with female customers. I haven't thought anything of it until now."

"Do you think he tried it on with Else?" I asked.

At that point something happened which you wouldn't believe if you read it in a story.

Someone who was passing our table, a man we both knew slightly, stopped to talk.

"I couldn't help overhearing, Craig, Christine. Sorry about my nosy ways but you see Anton was the name of a man I saw in here with a woman, about forty, black hair, Roman nose."

I stopped him before he said, "Roamin' all over her face" and bought him a Merlot.

By the time I returned, Micah had indeed established that it was probably Else. Our friend, (his name incidentally was Cedric. I think his parents hated him before birth.) had clearly listened in on their conversation.

"She gave him the brush off good and proper."

When Cedric had gone, Micah said to me, "Anton expected to get off with Else, she had agreed to meet him for a drink. So when she rejected his advances he repaired her computer by changing the 6502 chip to deliver his sinister message. We don't know that he then tried to poison her with LSD but if he wanted to 'control her mind' that would be a good way to start."

"We don't have any proof though." I said.

"That is where you come in," she said sweetly.

So it was that I found myself running a surveillance operation on the Tillotson house. Else had returned home but it was, Ben told me, unlikely she would ever return to work. She feared to go out of the house.

It was only a guess that Anton would try to attack but it was the only idea we had. Micah's cyber-skills came much later when the internet and mobile phones became her personal domain.

We spent some cosy evenings in the car waiting for something to happen so the time wasn't wasted.

"Did you see that?" Micah has eyes like a cat.

Eventually even my dim vision detected a figure in black approaching the back door. It was three in the morning so we guessed it wasn't a Jehovah's witness. We got out of the car as silently as possible.

The door had a glass panel and Anton, or whoever it was, tried to remove it with a screwdriver. They were so intent on their work that they didn't notice us. This was just as well.

The burglar screamed when Micah grabbed them and I appropriated the screwdriver. The scream didn't really sound like Anton but it awoke the inhabitants of the house and probably several others.

Ben opened the door and immediately took charge.

"Well well, Cindy Lane, what brings you round here at this ungodly hour? I'll take that," he said.

The final remark referred to Cindy's knife. Ben had a few words to say to me about not disarming her but that came later.

Cindy roundly abused us, Else and Anton in that order. 'Two-timing son of a whore' was the politest thing she said about him.

Else came downstairs and actually made Cindy a cup of tea. Then the whole story came out. Stripped of the foul language it was as follows:

Cindy worked for Computawares and she was Anton's lover. His flirting with female customers had been a laugh to start with, she said. Then it was an irritation. Finally it was intolerable. She knew Anton's designs on Else but did not know about her discussion with him in the Hare and Hounds. She convinced herself that Anton was going to leave her for Else.

Else patted her hand and just shook her head. The knife was still on the table but Else didn't ask what Cindy had intended to do with it.

Cindy had adapted the chip in the computer, it was "child's play" to her. The LSD was the next step in her plan and then the knife. A couple of 'uniforms', as Ben called them, came to escort her to the station.

"You are a pair of bloody amateurs, you should leave the likes of Cindy to the professionals. I know her of old and she has always had a violent streak. And what kind of buffoon leaves someone like her with a knife?" was all the thanks we got.

Micah and I drove away.

"You realise that Else could have been killed if we hadn't..." she began.

"Ben realises it too. That was why he was so angry," I said.

"We made a good team, Craig."

"Yes we did," I said modestly.

One last thing. Reader, I married her. Then, you already knew that.

# Murder in the Dark

"Murder in the dark" is a charming game for children in which the little darlings try to scare the living daylights out of themselves and each other. Why the adult members of the Atkins family decided it would be a good idea to play it was not known. Several bottles of booze were the prime suspects however.

Jenny Atkins gave a blood-curdling scream in the darkened room but that was all part of the game. The player with the ace of spades – the murderer – had touched her on the shoulder. The others laughed hysterically about this until the lights came on and they saw Jenny was in a state of shock and her hands were covered in blood.

The body of her husband, Jack, was slumped by the fireside with the poker protruding from his chest. There was no fire because they had central heating. The poker was a quaint relic of the past but a fatal one for Jack.

"Craig, you've got to come round."

"Certainly, Tommy, what's it all about?"

"There's been a murder. You must come."

"OK, Tommy. We'll be round as soon as possible but you must call the police and don't touch anything if you can help it."

"OK, Sarge."

That was Tommy all over. I hadn't been a sergeant for a very long time. And his name wasn't Tommy, it was Charles. He took the name "Tommy Atkins" as the archetypal soldier when he joined the regiment. The name was probably invented by the Duke of Wellington.

When we got to the house, we found the party-goers were gathered in the living room. They were not in a party mood. The front room had been left with just the corpse and the twinkling lights of the Christmas tree. Very festive.

Everybody was in a state of shock and explained shamefacedly what game they had been playing when the murder occurred.

"And I was the murderer," Sally Mikus, a next-door neighbour confessed. She held out the ace of spades she had drawn from the pack at the beginning of the game. You are not actually supposed to kill anybody but she probably knew that. She threw up into a waste-paper basket and we could see that the other guests were getting a little queasy.

"Coffee?" I suggested to Tommy and he took the hint.

Micah got down to business at once with her notebook. She refrained from using the word 'suspects', she inked it in later.

- Jenny Atkins, the victim's wife.
- Jeremy Mikus, neighbour, originally from Czechoslovakia, when there was a Czechoslovakia.
- Sally Mikus, his wife who was born in Durrington. Why she volunteered this fact we did not know.

- China Atkins, the victim's father.

- And of course, Tommy Atkins, the victim's son.

It is an interesting fact that people who are normally only too ready to talk, are reluctant to talk to us in such circumstances. So Micah spoke to the suspects in the kitchen while the others held a rather stilted conversation in the living room.

Everyone who had been blundering around in the darkened room had some blood stains on their clothing and the police would be wanting to take the clothes for evidence. What we noticed straight away was that the quantity of blood the unfortunate victim had shed was remarkably small.

Micah had the bad but quite useful habit of recording her conversations on her phone.

"Tommy, can you think of anyone who would want to kill your dad?"

"Isn't that the sort of question the police ask?"

"Do you always answer a question with a question?"

"Why do you ask?"

"This could go on, Tommy. We probably only have an hour before the police arrive. Anyway, you need to have thought about the question before they get here."

"OK, Micah, Mrs McLairy. The thing is I don't know anyone. Dad always said that his father, Grandad, would kill anybody on general principles but I think he was joking."

"Not the sort of joke you make about someone you love?"

Tommy laughed. "Well you have a point there but Grandad is a difficult or shall we say vicious old man. I imagine dad was getting his own back for his childhood. Grandad resented the fact that he had no power now. He tried to boss me around but dad would have none of it."

I thought our Tommy was going to be a very useful witness.

"China", as you probably know, is rhyming slang for "china plate, mate". China Atkins was not the most matey of people. He also had a hearing problem which meant everyone in the living room could hear his conversation with Micah and she had to speak up to be heard.

"I always have to spend Christmas with my worthless son and his bitch of a wife. Oh and that son of theirs."

"What brings you here?"

"My legs."

"I mean why do you spend Christmas with them?"

"It's my duty and it's their duty too."

"Mr Atkins, do you remember who suggested playing 'murder in the dark'?"

"None of my family. We don't hold with folk enjoying themselves. Foolishness. It might have been the whore from next door or that idiot husband of hers."

"How do you feel about your son being killed."

"No great loss, I expect."

He added a remark which silenced the crowd in the living room who heard every word, "He was doing rather more than coveting his neighbour's wife if you know what I mean. Now where is that coffee?"

While we were waiting for the police, it took them about an hour to get there, Micah went on to interview Jenny Atkins who was moving into the category of "prime suspect" after China Atkins' bombshell. Jenny spoke very quietly so I had to wait to listen to Micah's recording before I heard what she said. I noticed everyone in the living room was talking loudly about nothing except for China Atkins who was silent. Although he was never one to be full of the joys of spring, he seemed generally pleased with himself.

"Mrs McLairy, you must understand that Grandad is just a difficult character and he often says things he doesn't mean especially when he's hungry or he's had a drink or, you know, needs the toilet. You don't need to pay any heed to what he says."

"You heard what he said?" Micah asked.

"Everyone in the street heard what he said but it doesn't make it true. Now I come to think of it I can't think of a time when he has been cheerful. He did smile when Tommy fell over and cut his knee but that was a long time ago."

"So you don't think..." Micah said.

"No I don't think! If Jack had been 'playing away' I think the term is, his father would have killed him. Erm, sorry I mean, well one says these things but I don't want it taken literally. Grandad was a great one for duty and pride and it would injure the family name if anything like that got out."

Jeremy Mikus was the next suspect Micah interviewed. He slipped into German periodically but, as Micah said, at least it wasn't Czech because he originally came from Sudetenland where German is a common language. She has translated where necessary. Is there no end to her talents? Well she knows how to use Google Translate at least.

"I have no idea who suggested this silly game. I think it was just an excuse to get the lights out and have fun."

There was a pause while he thought about this.

"It didn't turn out like that of course."

"And, I hardly like to mention this but did you hear..."

"What that disgusting old man said? Of course I heard. I'm foreign but I am not deaf."

Another pause.

"You want to know if it is true?" He laughed. "How old fashioned you people are. You know all cats are grey in the dark."

"You think it is true?" asked Micah.

"I know it's true. We have no secrets from each other. Well none that I know of, that is." He laughed again. It didn't sound very mirthful. He lowered his voice.

"Of course Jenny didn't know anything about it. She would have engaged in a little wifely mutilation if she had. As for 'me old China' he talks of things he knows nothing about. I wonder what either of them would have done in a darkened room if they had been in possession of the facts and a poker."

The final rather ticklish interview was with Sally Mikus herself.

"Mrs McLairy, can I call you Micah?"

"Of course, Sally."

"Well this is to go no further, it is just between us."

"I'm not a priest, Sally, but unless you confess to a crime I don't have to tell the police anything. It would only be hearsay if I did."

Sally's sigh was audible.

"Did you know Jack well?" she asked.

"A little bit. Craig knew Tommy of course from his army days and we had met Jack and Jenny a few times," Micah replied.

"You see, Jack was a lovely man. He was caring and considerate not like, well, not like some people. We started out just having the odd drink after work at the Park View but somehow we just made a connection if you know what I mean. Anyway, he told me today that Jenny had found out all about us and our meetings. It is Tommy's army days that are bothering me. You know Tommy would have learned how to use bayonets and stuff like that and he was very protective of his mum. Nothing wrong with that as a rule but you can see the way my mind is going."

"I wish I'd never suggested that silly game but we were all a bit drunk and I wanted to be in the dark with Jack even if we weren't alone. It was exciting. Well, not how it turned out was it? I made sure I got the ace of spades you see and Jack got the Jack."

"And that meant?"

"He was the murder victim."

The police arrived. We left our details for no reason whatsoever and went off to the Park View for a meeting.

Micah got out her list of suspects. And we played over the recordings at a low volume.

"Tommy," she began, "I know you won't think anything bad about the lad but he was there, he was trained to kill and he was protective of his mother."

"I think he was protective of his family. It was to protect them and people like them that he joined up. That wouldn't include killing his father. What do you think this has done to Jenny?"

Micah subsided. She hadn't really liked Tommy as a suspect anyway.

"China. I think Tommy was right in thinking him a vicious old man but he was old and infirm. He made assertions about Sally but I doubt he had any facts, just malice. I would cross him off the list too."

"I'm not sure. I'm pretty old and infirm too," she had the good grace to laugh at that, "but I think this murder could have been the work of China. He called Sally 'a whore' and his son 'worthless'. Though to be fair he was pretty scathing about everybody. Including us, I imagine."

"Jeremy Mikus. Are we going to swallow the idea that he was happy about his wife sleeping with his next door neighbour?"

"Well they do things differently in Czechoslovakia."

"Come off it, Craig. It's not even a country and it is not so different either. Sudetenland is a pretty conservative place by all accounts."

"And how about Jenny with her 'wifely mutilation'? If she really knew.." I left the sentence unfinished and watched with satisfaction as Micah underlined Jenny's name.

"And can you think of a motive for Sally?"

"Not yet but leave her on the list in case we come up with something."

We ordered another bottle of Cabernet Sauvignon. Our list of suspects was largely unchanged.

The next morning I was awakened by a familiar noise. Micah had woken early to use her dark arts on the laptop. She saw I was awake and ordered tea.

"There wasn't enough blood," she remarked, when I brought in the mugs, "I have been browsing Inspector Tillotson's computer remotely and the postmortem reports. The victim was already dead before the encounter with the poker. An injection of insulin straight into the eyeball is the most likely means of murder. The killer must have been working by touch."

"So who could have touched him?"

"'All cats are grey in the dark,' to quote the odious Mr Mikus. Anyone could have touched him, I think. By the time he realised who it was, it would be far too late. And the levels of alcohol in the blood were off the scale."

"Alcohol, insulin overdose and a poker through the heart," I said.

"A lethal cocktail, you might think," Micah said.

The next thing we heard on *More Radio* was that Tommy had been arrested.

"What, I mean how do they think..." was as far as I got. Micah held her hand up for silence.

"Mr Charles Atkins has been arrested following an altercation with a neighbour, Mr Jeremy Mikus."

I went off to visit the Atkins family while Micah went home to follow the progress of the police investigation into the murder.

"Craig, thank goodness you've come. Tommy was out watering the lawn and that awful Jeremy was in his garden, up to no good I expect."

"What happened?"

"Well I don't know exactly what Jeremy said to Tommy but it was, you know, repeating what my father-in-law had said about Jack. Well, you know Tommy. He's a man of few words. He just turned the hose on Jeremy and Jeremy turned tail. It was funny to look at at the time and I have not had much to smile about."

"And then it seems the snake called the cops and they took Tommy in for questioning. They said it was assault."

"I'll have a word," I said.

Jeremy came to the door when I called round. He looked cleaner than I remembered him but I didn't like to say.

"You know that Atkins boy. I was assaulted by the young hooligan."

"Tell me what happened."

Jeremy told me.

In the end, after a couple of drinks, we agreed there was a funny side to it.

"I don't think the young ne'er-do-well should get away with it though."

"Of course not, Jeremy, he will get a caution from the police I'm sure. Perhaps we should all try to get along after the tragedy, don't you think?"

"Yes, Craig, I think you're right. Time for another drink before you leave. 'One for the road' as you people call it?"

I decided to be sociable. He decided it was probably all an accident. I said I'd tell Tommy to be more careful with the hose in future.

When I got to the Atkins' house, Tommy was back home and his mum was giving him the same sort of advice.

"Well, I'm off to the library," he said unexpectedly, "Every computer in the house is helping the police with their inquiries," he explained.

Micah had that look on her face when I got home. It suggested she had had an idea.

"The computers will probably do the police no good, she said, "The information will be on the email server if there is any information to find. I remember Jack once emailed you."

"Yes. He was cancelling a croquet game I remember. I think I can find it but it will only give me his email address not his password."

Micah looked at me pityingly and got to work on her laptop.

"Oh and can you ring Tommy and ask when his dad's birthday was?" she asked over her shoulder.

A surprisingly large number of people think "password" is a good password and since the email companies have started testing the complexity of passwords and rejecting simple ones, many have used significant dates as their password. One's own birthday is usually easy to remember and usually eight digits.

I had all the Atkins family birthdays written down for Micah and she thanked me profusely before letting me know that "Greytrees" was the name of their house and 66 was the number so the password hadn't been difficult to deduce.

She also said she was disappointed because she had an algorithm to find passwords she had been wanting to try out. I believed her.

"I had thought Jack would use some kind of code or even the end-to-end encryption of WhatsApp to contact his paramour but no, he used plain text emails. It is almost quaint," said Micah, adding, "some of the content of the emails was far from quaint. He decided it would be nice to spice up his messages to Sally and she reciprocated."

"No. You can't look at them. Think of your blood pressure. The one I think you should look at is this one."

'*My darling.*

'*Terrible news. The old bastard has been pouring poison into Jenny's ear about you. She put down the phone after a call from him and asked me point blank if we were having an affair. I think the expression on my face was enough to tell her the truth and we had the mother of all rows. I won't be able to see you openly in future without causing a disaster. I am sorry it had to end this way but we did have fun, didn't we?*'

"What do you think?" Micah asked.

"I think it's the most heartless 'Dear John' letter I ever heard. I take it 'the old bastard' is Mr Atkins senior." I said.

"From the context, yes. Old China didn't know anything but it seems his rumour-mongering was enough."

"It narrows the list of suspects," I said.

Micah crossed out all but two of the names on the list.

"I assume we are ruling out an interloper,"

"Grow up, Craig."

That night in the Park View we met someon
call 'Liam'.

"I'm glad I bumped into you. I think you're interested in the
Atkins case," said Liam.

"News gets around," I said.

"Well, I can tell you something."

"What would that be?"

Liam looked pointedly to the bar and then back at us. I went
to buy him a pint while he chatted with Micah. When I
returned, he said,

"I saw Jack and Sally in here," he looked around as if he
was suspicious of the other customers.

"When was this?"

"Well it was a while ago when they used to come in here
quite regularly for a drink after work. After that they must have
found somewhere else to spend their time together."

He could see I was underwhelmed by this information
because he added, "except for that one time."

He finished his pint in record time and I bought him another.

He lowered his voice, "They were talking very quietly but
intensely if you know what I mean. The wife and I used to
have rows like that so the kiddies wouldn't overhear anything
they shouldn't."

"And did you hear anything you shouldn't?" asked Micah
patiently.

ust one thing," he took another pull at his pint, "she said, ,ou should stand up to the old bastard. Don't be a coward.'. That sort-of ended the conversation and they didn't part on the best of terms."

Inspector Tillotson tells me he has to pay informants actual cash and then fill in a form about it. Our way works for us.

The next day was Sunday so I was in bed with the *Worthing Herald* crossword and Barker who had brought his lead in his mouth as a sort of hint when the phone rang.

"Look. Er, can you come round, Sarge?"

"So long as you call me Craig when I'm off duty, Tommy. I've been off duty for several years now."

"Right oh, Sar..Craig."

The kitchen was the heart of the Atkins home. That is where I found Tommy on his own and looking worried.

"Cup of tea?"

"Thanks. I see you're not using the tea pot."

"That's why I called you."

"The case of the missing teapot?"

"It's not missing , Craig, it's evidence. I'll start from the beginning. We only use the living room for visitors and I was in the kitchen when Mrs Mikus arrived and mum showed her into the front room and got me to make a pot of tea. I couldn't hear what they were saying and to be honest I wasn't interested. Then mum started shouting at Mrs Mikus. She was calling her a slut and a whore and a lot of other words I didn't know mum knew."

"You mean?"

"I mean there are some things you should not say and 'I've been sleeping with your husband." is probably one of them. I didn't believe what the old bastard said about dad and Mrs Mikus, nor did mum. Then suddenly she must've changed her mind."

"Anyhow, the next thing I heard was a scream and I couldn't tell who was screaming. It just went on and on and I just had to go in. Mum had chucked the tea pot at Mrs Mikus and it was half full at the time. Mrs Mikus's face was red. I mean literally, she had burns. I poured cold water on her because that's what you're supposed to do. She thought I was attacking her."

"By then mum had calmed down enough to call an ambulance. 'There's been an accident' was the party line on this and I don't know if I ought to go along with it."

"You only need to tell the police exactly what you saw. And in some bizarre set of circumstances it just might have been an accident. The fact your mum called the ambulance will count in her favour. Where is she, by the way?"

"Well the police have called her in for questioning and taken the teapot into custody and all."

I rang Micah with the information.

"It sounds like..."she began.

"Don't say a storm in a teacup. Don't even think it. It would be best if you go to Worthing Hospital Casualty Department. Whatever happens, Sally is in for a long wait and she might very well want to talk to an old friend. Mikus will be there, I imagine, but see what you can get out of her while he's, I don't know, fetching coffee. I expect Sally has had enough of tea," I said.

"And meanwhile you?" Micah can be quite sarky at times.

"Well I will be keeping Tommy company and taking Barker for a walk," I said.

"A walk to the nearest pub." It wasn't a question.

Barker is a very good assistant when I'm questioning suspects. It's a good dog, bad cop routine sometimes. With our Tommy though it was a fact-finding mission. I didn't realise what the most telling question was until much later. I inquired about the family, about work, it seemed Tommy was between jobs, Jack had been bringing in a decent wage and his insurance paid off the mortgage. Jenny was working at a local cafe for wages that made slavery look attractive.

"She is keen, well she was keen, to get into the kind of work Mrs Mikus does from time to time. Apparently there is an agency which employs people with nursing experience to care for terminally ill patients. It is all very zero-hours of course and the money is crap but it would be more useful than the cafe work and she wanted a second string to her bow, she said. I doubt if working with Mrs Mikus would appeal right now."

"Did you know anything about your dad and Mrs Mikus?" I asked.

"Aren't you supposed to say, 'I'm sorry to ask you this but...' or something?" he said.

"We are old friends," I said.

"You were a sergeant, I was a private. That's not the same."

"I'll get you another pint while you think about it. I don't have any rank now."

"No and you weren't one to pull rank anyway," Tommy said when I got back to our table. "I don't really know. I disbelieve anything the old bastard says or implies just because it's him saying it. So I didn't want to believe it but I've had a chance to think and there were all sorts of signs. Dad had work meetings that went on into the evening and he never had anything like that before. And then after he, you know, mum found he had been taking money out of the bank. We weren't skint but it wasn't petty cash either. It puzzled her."

I hadn't told Tommy but I had recorded everything on my phone. It's a habit I got from Micah. Personally, I trust my memory. She doesn't. I played the recording back to her.

"That's it then," she said and underlined one of the suspects.

"How was Sally?" I asked.

"Superficial. Not her personality, the burns. Tommy did the right thing pouring cold water on her. I suspect he enjoyed it but it did mean her burns were not as bad as they might be. The wait in Casualty was six hours though and then the doctors were a bit dismissive about her injuries. They would have preferred something life-threatening."

"We should visit her. Is she at home?" I asked.

For answer, Micah got her coat.

The Mikus family seemed surprised to see us but Sally was pleased to see Micah again.

After a bit of social chat, Micah said, "I want to tell you something about the murder. The police have found out the way Jack was killed."

Jeremy actually laughed. "A ruddy great poker sticking out of him must have been a bit of a clue."

"That is what we were supposed to think," Micah said, "but we know better than that, don't we Sally?"

I won't repeat the stream of unladylike abuse which came out of Sally's mouth but I think we can take it as a 'no'.

"You wanted to be in the dark with Jack," Micah continued.

"All cats are grey..." Jeremy began and then stopped.

"You see there were really only two suspects in this case. One works in a cafe where neither of the owners suffer from diabetes (I checked). The other provides caring services for old people and that includes insulin injections.

Old people can be quite absent-minded and taking a syringe and ampoules of insulin would have been child's play. Injecting straight into the eyeball is not easy and there are only so many people Jack would allow to touch his face in the dark."

Sally went berserk. It took both Jeremy and myself to keep her from Micah who sat calmly dialling Inspector Tillotson. He arrived in ten minutes. Micah handed him the email and provided him with the rest of the evidence.

"Very good," he said in front of the suspect, "it'll be enough to hang her."

He thought for a moment.

"Not that we do that any more of course, more's the pity."

"You're a right-wing dinosaur," said Micah.

"I don't think dinosaurs are into politics. They leave that to smartasses like you."

Sally didn't hang but she got a hefty sentence. Jenny's story about an accident was accepted and she served no time for assaulting her husband's murderer.

"Hell hath no fury..." I began as we read the story in the *Worthing Herald*. It made the front page..

"Stop there," said Micah.

# A Game of Chess

I gave up playing chess some years ago. I expect you are familiar with such moves as the Ruy Lopez opening and castling. The Ruy Lopez involves moving some of the chess pieces on the board. Castling is the same but with different pieces. The Park View still has the occasional game going on and I like to watch. I do this without commenting which seems the safest way. Chess is a game originally based on warfare. I had never heard of a game leading to fatalities until the Jameson/Buchanan match.

Harry Jameson and Oliver Buchanan were old rivals and the rivalry was none too friendly. Harry had been known to call Oliver a rank amateur and in my hearing Oliver called Harry a cheat, though how you cheat at chess I cannot fathom.

The game was due to take place at St Paul's in Chapel Street. Once a chapel, it has been a lively community centre for decades. It is also dog-friendly. Micah and I took Barker, who has a keen interest in the game and an even keener interest in doggy treats from the staff.

Both players were blindfolded and told their moves to the organiser, Daisy Simanovitch  who duly moved the right pieces on a large board. Oliver had insisted on this to stop any underhand dealing by Harry. It was the last jibe he was to make.

The players were on the stage of the main hall in St Paul's and the moves were projected onto a large screen for the audience. I later noted that neither player had anything to eat or drink during the game.

It was during the second match, after Harry had won one, that old Oliver suddenly pitched forward in his chair. His head struck the table and scattered the white pieces. Daisy rushed to help. Half a dozen people had mobile phones out and were phoning for an ambulance before he hit the ground.

"He looked a bit queer all through that game," said Daisy, "I hope to God he will be all right."

He was dead before he reached Worthing hospital. Micah hacked into their system because it represented more of a challenge than Inspector Tillotson's old laptop.

"Daisy was right," she said, "He would have looked more than a little unwell during the first game. Cause of death was a massive overdose of nicotine. The prime suspect is a doctored nicotine patch. He was trying to give up smoking..." she said, "for the good of his health, " she added without inflection.

Our next line of inquiry was unorthodox to say the least.

Mrs 'call me Daisy' Simanovitch approached me when I next dropped in to St Paul's for a latte and one of their excellent salads.

"Mr McLairy," she began and then hesitated.

"Yes, Daisy?"

"Well it's like this. You can say no if you like. It's entirely up to you, but some of us are getting together for a sort-of meeting. You might call it a séance I suppose but it is in memory of old Oliver. It was so sad, him dying like that. I was very upset. The get-together is here on Friday. I do hope you will come."

For anyone else, I would have pretended to have work to do but Daisy was one of those people you can't let down because she would take it to heart.

So the next Friday saw Micah, Daisy, Oliver's brother, Laurence and myself in a darkened room at the back of St Paul's with a medium who gave her name as Meg. This was probably a joke on her part echoing Mystic Meg. Either that or it was an unfortunate coincidence.

The room had been booked by Daisy under the guise of a craft group.

We all held hands and sure enough our 'Meg' started channelling Oliver. She even had his distinctive trace of a lowland Scots accent.

"This is a lovely place. I know my friends have been worried about me but this is a place of sunshine and happiness. I've met mum, Laurie, and she's very happy to be free of the pain that clouded her last years."

Before he could get talking about the choirs of angels, he interrupted himself to share a bit of wisdom from beyond the veil for Daisy.

"Is Daisy there?"

"Yes," she responded eagerly.

"You're still missing that gold brooch of yours. I can tell you this. You will find it in the bottom drawer of your chest of drawers in the bedroom."

"I've got a question, "I said, "Why did you sacrifice your bishop on the seventh move of your last game on earth?"

There was a pause. Then Oliver's voice continued, "I've gone beyond, Mr McLairy, I no longer think about those things."

"I'm losing him," said Meg in her own voice, "The spirits do not like disbelief, Mr McLairy, it drives them away."

As we were leaving, Daisy caught up with me.

"Did he really sacrifice his bishop on the seventh move?"

"Is the bishop the one like a large pawn with a slot in the top?" I asked.

"Yes."

"Then he didn't sacrifice it at all."

Daisy gave me a playful punch on the arm. It hurt but I think she got the point.

Nicotine patches are not only sold by chemists but old Oliver's local chemist seemed as good a place as any to start.

"Listen, Mr McLairy, I already done told the cops. This geezer came in here regular all right but all he bought was paracetamol, ibuprofen and those nicotine tablets, He never bought no nicotine patches. He said he could get them cheaper online. And a fat lot of good it did him."

Micah consulted her phone. She was Googling. I can always tell.

"There are a thousand online retailers for nicotine patches," she said.

"It is not good business practice for a firm to kill off its customers though."

"Tell that to the cigarette manufacturers," she said, a little sharply. I thought she had a point.

Micah sat for a few moments and then she used her computer to glean what information the police had come up with.

"The cause of death has been confirmed. Expert opinion is that it is not possible for a nicotine patch to be contaminated accidentally. If it were, the streets would be littered with the corpses of ex-smokers and nicotine patches might go out of fashion."

"The police are usefully describing this as murder by person or persons unknown," she added.

"Did Oliver have any enemies?" I asked.

"Apart from Harry? Well, he had a sharp tongue and no tact and diplomacy. The police have been unable to find anyone who thought of him as more than an irritation though. This crime required a fair amount of planning. I just don't buy the idea that anyone would go to all that effort just to remove an irritant. I think they would just avoid him or 'rise above it' as my mother used to say."

"Do they have any idea what assets he had, was he worth bumping off for his legacy?"

"His money, of which there was not much, went to the RSPCA. And no, I am not adding them to the list of suspects after 'person or persons unknown."

"So, nobody had a reason to kill him but somebody went to a lot of effort to do just that?"

"That is not helpful. Craig. Accurate but not helpful."

We were having breakfast at *The Black Cat* the following day. Micah stopped what she was saying because of the story on *More Radio.*

"Police are treating the sudden death of pensioner Simon Parker as suspicious. There are details which link his death to the death last week of Oliver Buchanan. Mr Buchanan was killed by an overdose of nicotine and Mr Parker, who collapsed and died in South Street, died in the same way."

"How safe are nicotine patches? Should we all be worried? Our medical correspondent, Simon Bates."

"Nicotine is a poison. Although people try to avoid the other poisons in cigarettes by using nicotine patches and vaping, these cases underline just how dangerous nicotine can be. It is virtually unheard-of for such a massive dose to be in a simple nicotine patch. That is why the police are treating this death as suspicious."

Between them, Micah and her laptop have an encyclopedic knowledge to rival Wikipedia. Something about the two murders had rung a bell and it wasn't long before she had the information at her fingertips. One piece was a letter in the Worthing Herald from five years ago from Oliver Buchanan

*"Dear Sir,*

*It was with some surprise that I found I was suffering from tennis elbow, since I last played the game in my teens.*

*On the advice of a friend, I sought the services of an aromatherapist who I will not name. Now aromatherapy is very relaxing and pleasant but for all the good it did my elbow I might as well have been sniffing the backside of a cow!*

*I reverted to a more conventional treatment of codeine and physiotherapy and that seemed to do the trick.*

*From now on, I will be leaving aromatherapy to the birds, specifically the gulls, and the gullible.*

*Yours Sincerely,*

*Oliver Fortescue Buchanan"*

"In itself, it proves nothing but when I take it together with this," she produced a recent copy of the *Worthing Journal.*

*"Dear Sir,*

*I was brought up in the days when doctors would recommend smoking for the nerves. Since then, you may be aware, the medical opinion has changed.*

*On the advice of a friend, I consulted a faith healer. The only practical result was that I found my faith sorely tested. The man (name removed) was a complete charlatan and I was angry with myself for being so gullible.*

*I will try something more practical in my war against the weed.*

*Yours sincerely,*

*Simon James Parker*

We presented our findings to Inspector Tillotson that evening over fish and chips at the John Selden. 'Poppycock' was the politest thing he found to say about them along with many other terms of disapprobation with which I won't sully the page..

Micah suggested, "I think it's time John Graham gave up smoking, don't you?"

John Graham is the occasional *alter-ego* I have used. I have a driving licence and bus pass bearing his name and my photograph thanks to Micah's forays onto the "dark web" as it is called.

First I wrote a blistering attack on homeopathy which the *Worthing Journal* was good enough to publish despite Prince Charles being a closet homeopath on the quiet. Then, as pension income and the odd client fee for the Durrington Detective Agency allowed, I started a regular order for nicotine patches from a variety of sources.

Micah converted half the kitchen into a laboratory where she tested the results for overdoses of nicotine while I prepared my legendary spaghetti bolognese and other delights in the other half.

In the event, Micah didn't need to put her chemistry skills (which she had updated with some useful YouTube videos) to the test.

Micah has a curiosity about the doings of our neighbours and she happened to be looking out of the window at the time the fourth packet of nicotine patches was delivered. Before I could do anything she was out of the door and haring across the grass. I reached the door in time to see her bringing down the courier with a passable rugby tackle.

I rushed out to separate the combatants. I turned over the courier and it took me a moment to recognise the face of the medium from my one and only séance. She looked far from happy. She grew less so when Micah produced a pair of handcuffs while I called the police.

We handed over the miscreant and the evidence when the boys in blue arrived.

It seemed not only was "Meg" (real name Sophie) keen to increase her clientele of the bereaved she was also a keen advocate of alternative therapies.

As Micah said, you can't get more alternative than murder, now can you?

# The Seagull

"He can't have been killed by a seagull."

"Yet he was."

I despise guessing games but they keep Micah happy when the mood is on her. We were sitting in the Park View enjoying the view and the Cabernet Sauvignon in equal measure.

The "Man Killed by Gull" headline in the *Worthing Herald* had brought on this speculation.

"It could have given him bird flu," I ventured.

"That would be likely if he had been plucking or preparing the seagull for lunch but he wasn't doing either of those things. First guess. Wrong." Micah looked very pleased.

I thought again.

"He could have been walking on the pier, distracted by a seagull stealing his chips or ice cream and fallen into the sea."

"It is very difficult to accidentally fall into the sea from the pier. The safety railings are too strong. Second guess. Wrong. You have one more guess."

I thought for a long while.

"It was a Seagull with a grudge, a Brighton and Hove Albion supporter. He was an Arsenal supporter and one thing led to another."

"That is a good guess. Thinking outside the box, very good. Wrong of course, but very good. That was your last guess."

"OK how did the seagull kill him?"

"It was a road traffic accident..."

"The seagull had a car?"

"Now be quiet and listen. The driver was distracted when a seagull smashed into his windscreen. The man drove off the road with fatal consequences."

"Seagulls don't do that."

"This one did."

"I don't believe it."

"Don't be Victor Meldrew. Just buy me a drink. A girl could die of thirst in here."

When I returned to the table with the drinks, Micah had dealt two hands for rummy and the rum business of the seagull was forgotten, for the time being.

Generally speaking, the forensic service do not carry out autopsies on seagulls. This is a pity and probably due to cut backs. I blame Theresa May.

The seagull in question had just been thrown away. I managed to retrieve it. There are advantages in having a doctor for a daughter although my request to Dorothy was one of the more peculiar ones.

"Why the devil have you got that revolting thing?"

"I have a question."

"Then take it to a vet, though I must warn you it is probably much too late. It looks like something the cat dragged in."

"Now come on, Dorothy, you know you used to enjoy cutting up dead animals, this is no different. Do you think you could just have a look while I get the dinner on the go?"

"I hope it isn't pigeon pie."

"Vegetarian Lasagne. No trace of pigeon," I said.

"I will have to take this blood-stained corpse away to have a good look at it. I can't give you an answer today."

I nodded and went to prepare the dinner. Micah looked at Dorothy sympathetically and poured her a drink.

In the event, she couldn't give me an answer for two weeks. She had enlisted the support of an amazed colleague to help out.

"Dad, I think there is something in your suspicions, not a lot but something. You see, this pigeon was dead before it hit the windscreen. Someone had very efficiently wrung its neck. Now would you like to come round to mine for some game pie?"

"There won't be any ..."

"Of course not. I have given it a decent burial."

"OK then, we will have a look at the calendar and ring you back."

The human victim's postmortem did not show anything inconsistent with a road traffic accident, according to Micah's researches. Nobody had wrung his neck, expertly or otherwise.

The phone rang. I have never received a phone call from the late Princess Diana and it was a brief moment before I realised it was Sekonda on the line. She runs a perfectly respectable business for men of a certain age who fancy a bit of royal company. She does not look like Princess Diana but she has the voice off perfectly. She also knew everyone in Worthing and their dark secrets.

"Craig. I understand you are interested in the death of Miroslav Karel?"

"The man who..."

"Well it wasn't the name of the seagull. It might interest you to know that he worked for Benevolent Chemicals."

"Not them again." I remembered a bruising encounter with their CEO, Marion Locke.

"Well, yes and no. Marion and her merry men were all offered a golden handshake to leave the company and keep their mouths shut when another company took over. I daresay it was a less benevolent one. The new CEO is Gustav Solinsky and he is a profoundly unpleasant man."

"There is a strong suspicion that Benevolent Chemicals have been experimenting on animals including seagulls. The animal rights activists have been targeting them a lot but the traffic has not all been one way. One animal rights activist was hospitalised by persons unknown. His name was Ken Groves.

"I think you might want to examine Karel's bank account. He was with Santander. I am sure the lovely Micah can do that. Anyway, give my regards to Micah and I won't expect any payment for this information until you have completed the case.".

I decided to take Mr Groves some grapes while Micah used her dark arts on Karel's bank account. His Facebook page obligingly gave her his date of birth which is often the key to numerical passwords.

"I don't like effing grapes," was Ken Groves' response to the gift. I was to find that 'effing' was his adjective of choice so I have omitted it from the conversation.

"What happened to you?"

"I was beaten with the proverbial blunt instrument by thugs from Benevolent Chemicals."

"Can you prove it was them?"

"Well of course not. They didn't give me their names and addresses. I gave the filth the description but it was dark. There were two of them, they wore balaclavas and they called me a terrorist. That is what suggested that Benevolent Chemicals was behind it. From their point of view everyone from the RSPCA to the RSPB are terrorists because they dislike the pointless torturing of animals."

"Pointless?"

"It has been possible to test drugs using tissue samples or computer simulations for decades. The results from animal testing are unreliable. You know if you tested arsenic on cats you would think it was harmless to humans and you'd be wrong. End of."

"Did you know Miroslav Karel?"

"'ere. Who the 'ell are you?"

I told him who I was and he told me to go forth and multiply. The nurse managed to look sympathetically at me and disapprovingly at him at the same time.

I went home to take Barker for a walk while Micah continued her researches. She had the laptop open and an old-fashioned notebook in which she was making some calculations about Miroslav's financial affairs.

After a walk across the rec, Barker was dog tired and he occupied the sofa for forty winks.

"I think the timeline works," I said, "Ken Groves could have killed our Miroslav and then been beaten in retaliation. He reacted to Miroslav's name like a guilty man but there is just one problem. I can't see an animal rights activist using a seagull as a weapon after wringing its neck."

Micah turned round.

"Miroslav was exceptionally well-paid for a driver. Someone has been depositing ten thousand pounds a month into his bank account. He hasn't won the lottery. I checked. However, almost all of the money in varying amounts was being paid into accounts in Alderney."

"His wife..."

"Jem Karel"

"..might be interested to know that. I was going to take her my condolences but I think a bit of journalism might be appropriate."

Micah looked out her imitation press card, which was remarkably like a real one. She took her phone to record the conversation. That's not exactly journalistic etiquette but then she is not exactly a journalist.

"Mrs Karel, I am Micah McLairy from the *Worthing Journal.* I am so sorry to hear about the death of your husband."

"The *Worthing Journal,* seriously? I always thought that was more of a one-man orchestra, band whatever. You are sorry about Miroslav and I expect you think I should be too. The truth is Miss McLairy, I hated the socks he stood in."

"I'm sorry to hear that."

"No you're not, it makes a good story." Jem Karel laughed briefly and then burst into tears.

Micah is very good at consoling weeping women (or men for that matter) and they were soon chatting like old friends.

"There is one thing that bothers me. Did you know that Miroslav was getting ten thousand a month and I am sorry to say that most of it wound up in bank accounts registered in Alderney."

"Who is Alderney?"

"It's an island. One of the Channel Islands."

"Well that is..."

Jem seemed lost for words. That state of affairs didn't last.

"I think that bastard was playing away. May his socks rot! On top of everything else I had to put up with. I hated his job. He never talked about it but I knew Benevolent Chemicals used to torture animals. I love animals. He knows I love animals so why take a job like that?"

"Things became silent between us," she continued, "We haven't spoken. And now he's dead and you come along and tell me he has some bit of fluff on the side. It's all too much, Micah. It's all too much."

"I didn't say he had a bit of fluff on the side, Jem, but he was playing away. Alderney is the centre for online gambling," Micah said.

Jem went into a stream of imaginative invective about her husband. She also moved up the list of suspects at the same time.

Benevolent Chemicals was a secretive company. The given reason was that its employees had been threatened by animal rights activists. They would not talk to us. Micah was able to hack into the computer of Inspector Ben Tillotson to find out the record of an interview with the CEO of Benevolent Chemicals, Gustav Slovinsky.

"Yes, Inspector, I have been blind from birth. I have congenital glaucoma. I have high hopes that our work here at Benevolent Chemicals will lead to a cure. It will be too late for me but think about the children, Inspector, think about the children."

"Did your work involve experiments on animals, seagulls for instance?"

"My work does not but I know that we employ strict guidelines and all our experimentation is within the law. The animal rights activists are the ones you should be interrogating."

"What was Miroslav Karel like as an employee?"

"Mr Karel had a past, let's just put it like that."

"I need more detail than that."

"You will have to talk to my ADC about that but it was only minor offences for which he has, as you might say, paid the price. We believe in second chances here at Benevolent Chemicals."

The second interview was with the ADC, Peter Graves. I cannot explain it rationally but there was something I instinctively disliked about his voice. Unctuous is not a word I use often but I will give it an outing to describe that voice.

"Inspector, do come in. How can we help you today?"

"You are the ADC to Mr Slovinsky?"

Graves laughed. If anything the mirthless laugh was worse than the voice. Now, I have never been tortured except by a dental hygienist  but I imagine a Gestapo officer laughing like that.

"Mr Slovinsky likes to use that acronym but actually I am his second-in-command."

"I see, sir. Mr Slovinsky referred me to you about the criminal record of  Miroslav Karel."

"Wouldn't the police have such records, Inspector?"

"Not if they were spent convictions for minor crimes a long time ago."

"Minor crimes a long time ago. Yes. And in Poland when Karel was a teenager. He was quite up front about his record when he applied for his job here. Benevolent Chemicals believes in second chances as I am sure Mr Slovinsky will have told you."

That laugh again. It was really beginning to grate.

"What was he like as an employee?"

"His work record was good. The useful thing about giving second chances is that employees know they have to be better than the rest if they are to keep the job."

"I see. What exactly did he do?"

"He was a driver."

"A good driver?"

"One of the best."

"So it seems strange that he died in a road accident."

"Exceptional circumstances, I think. Now I do have a lot of work on at the moment, Inspector so will that be all?"

"Thank you for your assistance, sir."

Inspector Ben Tillotson can make 'sir' sound like a threat and an insult rolled into one. I think it is a skill taught at Police College.

Micah didn't need any urging to start trying to hack into the computer system of Benevolent Chemicals. I know for a fact that she can penetrate the secrets of state agencies so the fact it was harder to hack Benevolent Chemicals was instructive in itself.

"Any luck?" I asked when I brought Barker in after a run around the recreation ground. That is to say he did the running and I applauded.

"Yes and no. I have got into their system and found one piece of very useful information but I find Peter Graves' activities both suspect and frustratingly obscure."

"Let's start with the useful information," I said.

"I have struck gold as far as Benevolent Chemicals is concerned. A disgruntled employee who was sacked at the behest of Mr Graves for insubordination. I have arranged for us to see him after dinner. His name is Gold too, Jamir Gold."

"And what has the slimy toad been up to?"

"Ah, Graves, yes. He goes onto a chatroom on the dark web during working hours it seems and that is suspect. However the conversation is all in code."

"I thought computers were designed to crack codes."

"You thought no such thing. Computers crack ciphers so HAL becomes IBM if you shift the letters one place in the alphabet. Many are more complex than that. However, Turing showed that they could be broken. Nobody can break a code."

"How come?"

"You know this, Craig. In a code whole words or phrases are replaced by other words or phrases. 'The birds are flying south for the winter' might mean 'we are about to conquer Poland' or 'meet me at eight and don't be late.'"

"At a push it might mean that the birds are flying south for the winter," I suggested.

Micah nodded.

"So the only way to break it is to get hold of the code book or beat the code out of the person who uses it, not that we would dream of doing that. Before you ask, Graves has numerous encrypted files on his computer. Decrypting them was relatively easy. They might tell us a lot about the financial dealings of Benevolent Chemicals but none of them is a code book. He must have it on an offline computer or even an old-fashioned notebook."

"Or he could keep it in his head."

"Unlikely but possible."

"Encrypted email to a bogus account?"

"I will look into that. Meanwhile, there is Mr Gold."

"Are we reporters this time?"

"That is probably best but we could be investigating the death of Mr Karel because ..."

"Disgruntled employees stick together?" I wondered out loud.

"Quite so. Although if I were getting an extra ten thousand a month I would be quite gruntled myself."

Jamir Gold lived in a terraced house in Salvington Road. This was easily in walking distance which was just as well because he had developed a taste for very cheap vodka and insisted on sharing it with any guests or, I suspect, just strangers he called in off the street. Nobody likes to drink alone.

"Mr McLairy, Mrs McLairy. I know just who you are or I wouldn't have let you in the house. I have been following the Durrington Detective Agency in the press for a number of years. I had to be sure you weren't animal rights terrorists."

"Well I stroke Barker occasionally but that is about as far as it goes."

"Who's a good boy then?" (Well he is sometimes). "I have got some Winalot biscuits here somewhere. Is he allowed them?"

"He'll be your friend for life I imagine, Jamir. That is an unusual name if you don't mind me saying so."

"Says the man who calls his dog, 'Barker'."

Barker usually breaks the ice and he seemed to be succeeding here. Before we could ask any questions, he said,

"There is something you ought to know about Benevolent Chemicals. They do experiment on animals it's true but the biggest animal in the place is the 'Number Two', as he likes to be called. We think he doesn't know what a 'number two' is in schoolboy slang. I made up my mind to tell you about a game Graves plays with his office staff."

"He only plays it when they are working late and alone with Graves. It is called 'the dice game'. You throw a dice and each number is assigned to a forfeit. To start with the forfeits are trivial but as time goes by they become more extreme. The player has to do something painful or humiliating. Throw a one and you have to shut your hand in the drawer, throw a three and you have to insult your mother. That is the kind of thing."

"Anyone who won't play the game is 'not one of us' or 'not a team player' and is sacked on the spot. There is no union allowed at Benevolent Chemicals and we are all on zero hours contracts so that sort of draconian working practice is commonplace. The seagulls weren't the only ones suffering."

"Did you know Miroslav Karel?"

"Did I? Have another drink and I will tell you something very interesting about him."

We did as suggested.

"There came a time when the computer systems of Benevolent Chemicals were all down. I noticed Number Two was getting quite agitated about being separated from his computer. He made a phone call. It was one of my jobs to log all the phone calls into and out of Benevolent Chemicals. For want of a better word we were a bit paranoid about security. So I have a record of the phone number that he rang."

He handed me a piece of paper and looked round at the walls as if they might have ears. They didn't.

"I can tell you exactly what he said. 'I don't want any songs this Christmas. Can you deal with this matter for me? An unfortunate accident perhaps?'"

I looked at Micah. She looked at me.

"Do I take it that this was..."

"It was a week before Miroslav Karel died. And it was a crude pun on his surname. It was also six months away from Christmas."

Using an online reverse telephone directory told us that one Jimmy Dexter had been careless. Instead of using one of the burner phones so beloved of crime dramas, he had used his home phone. In his defence, perhaps, the fact that an encoded chat was his usual means of communication had led to this sloppiness.

We were no nearer proving that the Graves and Dexter partnership was responsible for the murder but it did give us an idea of where to look.

Micah looked after Barker while I spent a damp evening sitting in the car outside Dexter's address. I was rewarded with a photograph of sorts. Some of the apps on my phone turned it into a rather better version.

It was time to visit Ken Groves again. I did without the grapes and tried a couple of cans of lager.

"I'm sorry I was a bit abrupt last time," he said, eyeing the cans.

"That's OK. I know the men who did this to you wore balaclavas but I have a photograph which I would like to show you."

"Of a balaclava?"

"No."

I showed him the photograph.

"Oh yes, everybody knows old Jimmy Dexter. He's as nasty a thug as you will ever come across. You're going to need to watch your step, Mr McLairy, if you are going to mess with the likes of him."

After we polished off the cans, I was 'Craig' and possibly his best mate in the whole world.

I asked around and the phrase "nasty piece of work" cropped up in my conversations with Sekonda and old Ben Tillotson. Ben said our evidence of an overheard phone call was of no use but if we could crack the code of the chatroom then we were in with a chance.

The police could requisition the transcripts of the private chats. I did wonder briefly how many people who use chat rooms knew that useful piece of information.

I continued surveillance of Mr Dexter. Sometimes I openly walked Barker down the street but most of the time I kept out of sight.

Nobody shared the house with him. Sekonda told me that there had been girlfriends at various times but they did not last long.

Jimmy Dexter had his own CCTV system and a burglar alarm. He was a man of nocturnal habits and often left the house around midnight, returning in the morning. He was probably supplementing his income from Benevolent Chemicals with a bit of burglary but that was not our prime concern.

"He has several firewalls," Micah said after her first attempt to hack into the Dexter computer.

"Does that make it safer?"

Micah looked at me pityingly and slowly shook her head.

"The more conflicting anti-intrusion measures you have on a computer, the less secure the information is. The trouble is that apart from a collection of porn which I won't bore you with, there is precious little on the computer.

"Some files are encrypted in an amateurish sort of way but they are just names and addresses of animal rights activists. Some of them are marked with a cross. Since Ken Groves is one of them, we can guess what the cross is for. It might be useful evidence but ..."

"No code book," I ventured.

"That must mean either it is all in his head or in a physical book. How are you at breaking and entering?"

"You know the answer to that."

Micah smiled.

I don't possess an old service revolver but Micah provided me with a taser she picked up from an American website for a modest sum. I suspect we looked like friends of Jimmy Dexter in the balaclavas we wore for the raid on his premises. I left the CCTV and childishly simple burglar alarm for Micah to deal with.

She searched the living room thoroughly.

"It's no use," she said, "there is neither hide nor hair of that code book."

"Craig, why are you browsing his porn collection?"

"I've got an idea."

"You've got quite enough ideas."

"What about this?"

I enlarged one of the lurid pictures and there, sure enough was a block of binary that had no business being there.

"Let's get out of here."

I downloaded the picture onto a pen drive. This was unnecessary but I didn't want to think the night was completely wasted.

We met Ben Tillotson in the John Selden.

"I'm a bit old for dirty pictures," he said once I'd put a pint of Harvey's within his grasp and showed him the data.

Micah coughed.

"This," she handed over her notebook, "is a translation into plain English. It was a code within a code. The binary was a simple cypher but it provided all the information for the code. The conversations between Graves and Dexter after the murder of Miroslav Karel show complicity. Dexter was highly amused that a dead seagull had put paid to an employee of Benevolent Chemicals who intended to blow the whistle on their dirty dealings."

"So you have killed two birds with one stone," Old Ben seemed grimly amused.

Graves and Dexter were convicted of murder with a number of other counts of intimidation and violence to be taken into consideration. Benevolent Chemicals went out of business. Seagulls nest in their old premises.

# One Man and His Machete

There was a time when a decent burglar (if there is such a thing) would wait until the family was out or at least try to burgle the house quietly without disturbing anybody. Not any more. Machete Man will break into a house, usually with a friend; he will demand money, cards and pin numbers and he will start hacking off body parts if he doesn't get them.

Of course, this couldn't possibly happen in Durrington. Except that apparently it had.

"A couple in Dartmoor Close, Durrington were robbed by two thieves wielding machetes who broke into their house and demanded money with menaces on Monday night between the hours of ten and eleven. The police are appealing for witnesses," *More Radio* announced.

Micah and I were sitting in the Black Cat having breakfast.

"It would have been dark and the street lights are coming on later and later as part of an economy drive," Micah observed. "I live here because it is a nice place where this sort of thing does not happen. Be quiet, Craig."

I hadn't thought of saying anything at this point.

"It's not our case obvs, but we can't let this go."

She had picked up the use of "obvs" for "obviously" from a niece and I was quietly waiting for her to drop it again.

"So what can we do?"

"Well we could at least ask around."

For me "asking around" usually meant a phone call to Sekonda. To Micah it usually meant illegally accessing police information. Still, each to their own.

That evening as we were tucking into spaghetti bolognese (my spag bol is of surpassing excellence if I say so myself) we compared notes.

"The man's name is Lech Bocks. That is to say the victim's name. I don't know Machete Man's name. Not yet." Micah began.

"He was bullied at school by people who wanted to see if he could box. Children can be very cruel," I added.

Micah nodded.

"His partner is called Tayla Match." Micah was making notes.

"Actually his wife. She just kept her maiden name for obvious reasons. Too many jokes just begging to be told.," I said.

Micah also had their dates of birth and various other data.

"Machete Man had a strong Glaswegian accent. His accomplice was the silent type. Average height, average clothes, average everything really. The balaclavas were knitted."

"Anything else?"

"Their bank account confirms that they took out all the money from it on the day of the robbery," Micah paused.

I waited and eventually she continued.

"I looked back over the last few months. The lion's share of their incomes from the County Council (Tayla) and from Barclays (Lech) were transferred to a numbered account. The name of the account-holder was a money-lender, Simon Dangerfield. His rates of interest would make Shylock's eyes water."

"Does that make him a suspect?"

"Yes and no. If they defaulted on a payment then he would have to make an example of them. On the other hand, if they kept up the payments he would be the last person to rob them. Although he is a nasty little man."

I "accidentally on purpose" bumped into Lech at the Crown. It is not a pub I would frequent for choice. The carpets are filthy.

I couldn't take Barker because they ban dogs. In any case I think he would need a bath after contact with that carpet. Nevertheless we did discuss dogs. Lech owns a Staffie called Jaruzelski. Jaruzelski had a number of little habits which were cute or irritating depending on your perspective.

We went on to talk for a while about Brexit and the state of the nation but he was bound to mention his recent experience as an example of the latter.

He did.

"You know about my run in with the Machete Man? It's a sign of how this country has gone to the dogs. You ought to feel safe in your own home." He raised his voice and got sounds of approval from other customers who had clearly heard the story too.

"Yes I saw it in the papers. It's appalling. Have the police got anywhere?"

"What do you think?" he asked.

I kept my thoughts to myself so he continued, "It's like that time the police toilets were stolen. They've got nothing to go on. I didn't get a proper look at the criminals. They seemed a couple of average guys in terms of height and weight and what have you. I never saw their faces because they wore those knitted balaclavas. They were dressed in black except their trainers which were both white and both identical."

"You can see I've had to go through all this for the cops, for all the good its done. Someone can just break into your own home and threaten you and then get away with it."

I offered to buy him a drink and he ordered an improbably large whisky before taking his leave.

"He's had a terrible time," one customer confided to me, "been too frightened to come out of the house so it's good to see him here. He probably needed that shot to summon up the courage to go home."

Our next information about Machete Man, as the papers were calling him despite the fact there were two of them, came from an unusual article on the Worthing Herald website.

"Officers of Adur and Worthing Council got more than they bargained for when a case of fly-tipping was reported in a Durrington car park. The item was a refrigerator but when they opened it they had to call the police immediately. A body had been cut up to fit into the space. The officers have been off sick with stress since the finding yesterday."

"Inspector Tillotson has appealed for calm. He would like any information about the dumping of the refrigerator which police believe must have been by the murderer or murderers. He confirmed to us that the mutilations could have easily been the work of a machete and repeated his appeal for the public not to panic."

"There is as yet no information about the identity of the corpse but DNA, fingerprinting and dental records are all being consulted. The police are also interested in any reported or unreported missing persons."

"Is this the work of the Durrington Machete Man?"

The following day there was an interview with the man who reported the fly-tipping. Mr Baron was unable to provide much information.

"Well I think it was Saturday but it might have been Tuesday because I always like to take the dog for a walk on those days but it might have been Wednesday. Any day really. I just saw the fridge. I can assure you I know nothing about the...well you know...inside it or I wouldn't have reported it. I like to keep myself to myself you know."

"Nowt so queer as folk," Micah commented on this, adding, "I think we might have a little chat with Mr Baron and see if we can clarify his reminiscences."

The "little talk" wasn't straightforward. We took Barker because he is good at breaking the ice. Unfortunately, Mr Baron's shihtzu Oswald was having none of it and set up a barking which could have wakened the man in the fridge.

"I've said all I'm going to say."

He started to shut the door. Micah said, "Ah, Mr Baron I think you might have been traumatised on finding out the contents of the fridge and you might be entitled to compensation."

It's a lovely word, 'might' isn't it? All sorts of things might happen so Micah wasn't actually lying, she wasn't exactly telling the truth either but it did the trick.

"I suppose you'd better come in."

"It would help us considerably if you could just show us the place where you saw the fridge and then we can come back and fill in some forms. We need a few details." Micah smiled.

"I'll show you. I'll bring Oswald. He needs a walk and he won't bark at your dog so much if they are both on common ground and not in Oswald's home."

We walked the short distance to the car park. It was bordered by a small area of trees and there was a fair amount of rubbish strewn around.

"You see what I mean. People treat this as a tip. The council are always coming round to clear it, mainly because I ring them up. As you can see it is a labour of Sisyphus. All this rubbish has been left here since the council cleared the area a couple of days ago."

"The fridge was just here. It was lying on its back. I suppose the door might have come open if it were upright and that would have been ghastly. I reported it to the council."

"Was this the same day?"

"No it was the day after."

"Do you ever watch the TV? Did you see ' Line of Duty'?"

"Come to think of it, I did watch it."

"Was that on the same day as you found the fridge."

"No it was the day before."

Micah made a note in her notebook. We talked about 'Line of Duty' on the way back and then Micah produced some official-looking claim forms which she filled in for Mr Baron. We had the date, the time and the fact that he had never seen the fridge there before so we could pinpoint when it arrived at least.

"Do you have any ideas about who might have dumped it?"

"No, I told the police that I hadn't seen it being dumped. It would have taken quite a sturdy vehicle to carry the weight though."

When we got home there was more news on the Worthing Herald website.

"The body that was found in a refrigerator in Durrington has been positively identified by DNA as that of Mr Simon Dangerfield, a prominent local businessman. He has no family and therefore he had not been reported missing. His business associate, Mr Eric Green, was unavailable for comment but it is understood that Mr Green will be taking over the business."

"It couldn't have happened to a nicer bloke," Micah said, "I suppose I'll have to take him off the list of suspects. He couldn't have chopped himself up into fridge-sized bits. However, apart from the people who owed him money, my main suspect would be this Green character. He is taking over a dirty but lucrative business."

"The people who owed him money?" I asked.

"We will have a devil of a long list and I have a sneaking and quite unprofessional sympathy for anyone who kills a money-lender. Green is a different case of course. We will see if he will talk to us. We could be shopping around for a loan."

"Those blood-suckers are not really for people who can afford to shop around," I began.

"Any better ideas?"

For Micah my silence implies consent so we got Green's address from a card in the newsagent's window and went round to see him.

Mr Green lived in one of the posh houses in High Salvington. He looked the part of a businessman but there was something unpleasant about him which gave away what a nasty business he was involved in.

"Now then, Mr McLairy, Mrs McLairy, can I offer you a cup of tea?"

We accepted the offer and sat down on seats to which the misery of Mr Green's clients seemed to cling. That may have been my imagination. In fact Micah tells me it definitely was.

"Now I know full well you were not interested in borrowing money from me. I am sure the Durrington Detective Agency has plenty of resources so that set me thinking about what you were here for," he began.

"You know of my unfortunate partner's demise. I can assure you that I have a perfectly good alibi for the time of the murder. Still there is nothing so suspicious as a good alibi, eh Craig?"

His laugh was not pleasant to listen to.

"How did you two get on?" I asked.

"He was a good boss. I had no complaints on that score. I could wish his records were in better order so I could continue to provide the same service to the community as Mr Dangerfield but there it is. I am sure there will be new clients to take the place of Mr Dangerfield's list."

"The list is missing?"

"As I said, don't make me repeat myself."

"He kept it on him?" Micah asked.

"He was old fashioned like that. All records in a little black book. It is sadly missing which will not make this changeover easy, Mrs McLairy. Now if you have no other questions, I am a very busy man."

"A supremely nasty man but can you see him wielding a machete?" I asked as we made our exit.

"He would have got somebody else to do that," Micah said, "I can imagine him giving the order though."

An hour later, Micah looked up from her laptop and shook her head.

"He makes no use of social media, he does not use online banking, he does not have an email account. If he has a computer it is not connected to the internet and he only uses his mobile phone for calls." she said.

"A complete dinosaur," I said.

"Well he should suit you then."

Barker always likes a ride in the car so I took him up to High Salvington. I parked at some distance from Mr Green's house. This was going to be a long job.

I was a bit surprised when my phone started vibrating.

"Hello, McLairy, Green here. Listen, High Salvington is quite a nice neighbourhood. We don't want you and your smelly Durrington dog around here. Just thought I'd tell you the police are on their way and if there is any more stalking from you I will have an Anti-Social Behaviour Order slapped on you and have that dog put down. I'm quite friendly with the magistrates around here, you know. Now be a good fellow and buzz off."

I didn't know how much of that was bluff but I didn't hang around to find out.

"Sekonda?"

"I see you are looking into the unfortunate demise of Dangerfield."

How Sekonda knows these things I don't know. I suspect witchcraft but she has been very useful to us in the past.

"Do you know anything about Eric Green?"

"I know enough to keep well away from him. He isn't violent. Not now anyway but in his youth he was a vicious tearaway. He was inside for actual bodily harm for two years but usually his victims refused to prosecute because they were frightened of the consequences.. It was his girlfriend who was prepared to give evidence."

"Do we know why?"

"We found out six months later when the girl died. Beatings from Green had accelerated her death by several years, according to Dr Winter. He was a half-decent doctor in those days remember. The windbag years came later. Green doesn't need to do the heavy side of the job any more. He has a young Walt Alderman for that. He drinks at the Egremont and he usually drinks alone. I hope that is useful."

"As ever, Sekonda. Shall we say fifty quid's worth of useful?"

"You're too generous. No I take that back. Fifty is just right."

Sekonda laughed.

"My mother told me never to talk to strangers," was the disappointing response from Walt Alderman when I caught up with him in the Egremont

"I wondered if you fancied a game of cards," I suggested.

"For money?"

"You can't play cards for money in a pub without a gambling licence," I said, taking out the pack of cards.

"What's the point then?"

I tried my last resort. "Fancy another?"

It usually works.

We settled down with our drinks and I eventually got him playing a game of rummy. He was very bad at it. I let him break the rules by taking back a few cards he had unwisely discarded but he was still bad at it.

We talked about Brexit and whether it would ever come to anything and the state of the country. This seemed as good a way as any of introducing the body in the fridge.

"Did you hear about that guy whose body was found in a fridge?"

"No," was his surprising reply.

He read a text message on his phone and suddenly smiled at me like an Alsatian who wanted me for dinner.

"Oh," he said, "I know all about you now, Mr Craig McLairy. Thanks for the drink but you can run along now and take your cards with you."

He threw his hand on the floor. I left it there. I wasn't going to get within kicking distance of him.

When I got home, I could tell something was wrong. Micah doesn't look stricken by qualms often.

She asked a few perfunctory questions about Alderman and nodded absent-mindedly when I replied.

It was over the shepherd's pie that she decided to unburden herself.

"You know Lech and Tayla claimed to have been robbed in their own home. They took all the money out of their bank account to give to the robber and that meant they couldn't pay Dangerfield."

I noticed her use of the word "claimed" and nodded.

"Well there's more to it than that. They could stall Dangerfield if they said they had been robbed but not indefinitely. He would demand his pound of flesh soon enough and no sob stories would stop him."

"Do you think they weren't robbed?"

"I know they weren't. I have been keeping tabs on their bank account. It is surprisingly easy. The bank should be more careful. However the point is that all of the stolen money has been returned."

"The man with the machete?"

"A work of fiction but one that became real after the event. The most likely explanation is that they chopped up Dangerfield, either separately or jointly. My money is on jointly because of the logistics of chopping up a body and putting it in a fridge."

"Well, we should hand this information over to Inspector Tillotson asap." I said without much hope that Micah would go along with this.

"They killed a money-lender."

"And you agreed it was unprofessional to let the nastiness of the victim prevent us pursuing the killer."

"It wasn't our case, Craig. We didn't have to do anything about it. And the means I used to get the information were illegal. You know what this means."

"It means we can't hand the information over to the police because they can't use the evidence."

"They can apply for a court order to investigate the bank accounts, but they have no reason to investigate the Bocks family. I'm sorry, Craig, we will have to leave the police to work this out for themselves."

Within six weeks, Lech Bocks confessed to his crime, gallantly absolving Tayla of all blame. She had in fact departed from the country. A clever lawyer tried to argue that the balance of his mind was disturbed. The jury concluded, however, that you don't need to be insane to want to chop up a money-lender.

In prison, Lech wrote a bestseller about his experiences. The profits were donated to Citizens' Advice.

# The Body Snatchers

Few things are worse than losing a pet. The sadness is made worse by the lack of understanding of friends and work colleagues. This indifference is exemplified with the statement "It was only a pet," which makes the owner want to scream at the lack of understanding that implies.

Missing a pet is just the same as missing an old friend who never criticised, was always pleased to see you and forced you to go on walks if the pet was a dog. You even miss the **smell** and that is hard to believe since it was often something of a drawback in your relationship.

The Bolton family had an additional and macabre twist of the knife after they lost their spaniel, Prince. We heard about it on *More Radio.*

"A Goring couple were shocked to find that they had been visited by body-snatchers. The resurrection men had made a visit to the Bolton back garden at dead of night. Mr Zak Bolton takes up the story,"

"I didn't believe my eyes, I shouted to Emmy, that's Mrs Bolton, to come out and have a look. The rose bush was lying in the middle of the garden. It was a lovely rose bush but more to the point we had planted it as a memorial to our beloved Prince."

"Prince?"

"He was the loveliest spaniel you ever saw. No fuss, no barking, big loving eyes. A prince among dogs he was. We buried him in the rose bed and we bought the rose specially for him, it was a blue moon rose with rather large blooms. And the body, the body."

"Take your time Mr Bolton."

"Well I just hope they catch whoever stole Prince's body and lock him up and throw away the key. If you do something like this to an animal, what are you doing to the humans who are left behind? That's what I'd like to know."

"There are a lot of things I'd like to know," Micah said after we had listened to this broadcast. She started to make a list.

- How old was Prince?
- When did he die?
- How did he die?
- How are the Boltons coping?
- Did they have any enemies?
- Could it have been kids?

"And then I want to catch the blighter," she said.

I nodded.

"Craig, I've done a search online and there is a magazine called *Pets We Have Loved* and they are interested in a freelance account of the Prince story although they couldn't promise publication."

"I think we will both go and take Barker. It's a bit of psychological warfare, a nice married couple with their dog."

We called on the Bolton family and sure enough they were fussing over Barker almost before we were through the door. We let them get on with it and start the interview in their own good time.

"Do you mind me asking, how did Prince die, Mr Bolton?"

"Call me Dale and this is Emmy, we don't stand on ceremony here. In answer to your question, we don't know. You see we thought he was a fit and healthy dog but he just died. It looked a peaceful death. We think he must have been snatched from our back garden."

I will mention now that the Bolton back garden was hardly a place in which you could lose yourself or even a small dog. I think there must have been a moment of carelessness for which the Boltons had been beating themselves up ever since.

"Where was he found?" Micah asked.

"It was over in the car park. At first we thought he had been poisoned. You do hear such dreadful things don't you? But a trainee vet who is also a neighbour, Mr Stevens, had a look at him and he was at a loss to say exactly how he died but he ruled out any known poison. That was like a crumb of comfort but not much of one."

Emmy Bolton was close to tears. I wasn't happy about bringing up these memories and I could tell Micah wasn't either.

"How old was Prince?"

"He was five. We'd had him since he was a puppy. We've got some photos."

We spent a good half hour reminiscing over the photos. We got a good picture of Prince's personality. The chance that he had attacked someone and been killed in retaliation was very slight. He was just not that kind of dog. Dale and Emmy would say that of course but they had impressed us as an honest couple. We have seen enough of the other kind to judge.

The digging up of the corpse had brought their feelings about Prince to the surface as well.

They shook their heads.

"To start with we thought the death was 'just one of those things' you know, things we can't explain," said Dale.

"But digging up the body was just awful and malicious. So the death probably wasn't er, well it must have been deliberate otherwise I can't understand any of it," Emmy said.

"Do you have any enemies?" Somebody had to ask and it was me.

Dale Bolton looked at me and considered for a moment.

"I have thought about this. I can honestly say that I didn't make enemies."

"What about those kids?" asked Emmy.

Dale Bolton actually laughed.

"There were some kids and they were making a devil of a racket around midnight so I went out to have a word. Prince came with me. The young tearaways actually asked me if they could stroke him so I don't count them as enemies. They might not like me much but they wouldn't have done anything to Prince."

We begged a couple of photographs from them for use with the article. Micah actually wrote it up and got all of twenty pounds for it in the end.

I asked her what she thought and she said in an abstracted way, "peaceful death" and went off to consult her friend Google.

Later she came into the lounge with a thoughtful expression.

"Are we assuming that the body-snatcher and the killer are one and the same?" she said.

"It doesn't look like natural causes although it was apparently peaceful. If they are one and the same..." I said.

"Then the resurrection was intended to destroy the evidence of the killing. Unsurprisingly they don't do autopsies on pets so we only have the word of Mr Stevens that poison was not used. We will need to talk to him. If we can find the noisy teenagers that would be a bonus. They must have disturbed other neighbours too."

"Let's do a house-to-house then," I suggested.

Micah looked at the persistent drizzle and she seemed less than enthusiastic but I think she craved action even if it didn't have much chance of success.

Mr Stevens, according to the police computers Micah had been perusing, had not been interviewed by them so he was rather surprised to see us.

"We are working on an article for *Pets We have Loved* and we have already spoken to Dale and Emmy Bolton..."

"Who's a good boy then?"

This was addressed to Barker. As ever he had done an excellent job of PR for us.

"I hope you don't mind if we talk out here, it's dryish under the porch and my Fluffy does not take to other dogs much, or indeed at all."

"It was a terrible business about the body being stolen. Adding insult to injury?"

"Dale asked me if Prince had been poisoned. Sadly I have seen too many cases of poisoned pets and Prince showed none of the symptoms. What I can't tell you is what he did die of. Just a minute, do you mind if I fetch a biscuit for ..."

"Barker," I said, "neither he nor I would mind at all."

Fluffy started barking at that point and Mr Stevens spent a while in pacification activities.

"Anyway that's all I know," he resumed. "It wasn't poison. I would stake my reputation on it. You see there would be vomit. The body tries to reject poison, usually too late of course but there was no sign of that."

"Did Fluffy get on with Prince?" Micah asked.

"Well they had the odd bark-off but yes I think they were used to each other. She would bristle a little when Dale and Emmy came round but she settled down well enough."

"One other thing," said Micah, "Dale said he went out to quieten down some youngsters do you remember the incident?"

"I sleep like the dead as a rule so all I know is what Dale told me. It seemed a minor incident from what he said and the lads went away. One of them was local, a Terry Smethwick. He is the son of Councillor Smethwick and usually a good lad by all accounts. I hope he isn't in any trouble. It was just high spirits."

Our inquiries in the other five houses in the close showed that the neighbours had heard the disturbance but had been loath to intervene. One of them said that he was on the point of going out and telling the youngsters 'what for' when Dale dealt with the matter and he didn't have to. I noticed his wife had a sceptical expression during this narrative.

Councillor Smethwick's son was our next person of interest. We knew of Councillor Smethwick of course. He was such a well-loved local character that people who detested politicians in general and Tories in particular still made an exception of him. If you needed help, you went to him and he would do his best for you regardless of who you voted for and regardless of what the Tory Party told him to do.

We were thinking about how to approach young Terry when the *Worthing Herald* arrived.

"LOCAL COUNCILLOR DIES SUDDENLY" was the headline. The story continued,

"The death of Councillor Smethwick has puzzled detectives. All the indications were that the councillor had drowned except that the body was dry, there was no water in the lungs and he was seated in a chair in his living room."

"Councillor Tony Smethwick leaves behind his son, Terry Smethwick, his wife, Theresa Smethwick and his invalid father also called Anthony."

"Tony has been praised by his political allies and opponents, church, mosque and synagogue leaders and the members of the general public in his ward of Durrington. He will be sadly missed both by his family and the community."

Micah took a moment to digest this before saying, "It is time we went to pay our respects, don't you think?"

I did think.

By chance I had met the councillor when some of our anti-social neighbours had decided to build a hideous extension. Councillor Smethwick had offered his assistance and fought tooth and nail against the planning department. I didn't blame him for the fact that they were too pig-headed to understand.

Although he represented Durrington, his home was in the posher area of High Salvington. It was easy enough to spot because it was festooned with flowers from well-wishers.

The door was opened by Mrs Smethwick. She was red-eyed.

"Well it was very nice of you to come, Mr McLairy, Mrs McLairy, er..."

"Barker."

"Of course, Barker, good to see you," she shook his proffered paw.

"It was such a shock, finding Tony like that. He was sitting in his favourite chair," she indicated the chair with a gesture but didn't look at it, "I thought he was asleep but he wasn't breathing. I tried the CPR I learnt at the WI but it was too late for any of that."

"He seemed very peaceful," she added. I looked at Micah.

Micah made a gesture which is hard to describe but I translated it as "Yes I heard that now be quiet and let me think."

The house was old. So much so indeed that the living room even had an old disused gas mantle as a feature although the light was provided by sconces at the side of the room with electric lights.

"Now I have the police trampling all over the place and they are insisting on an autopsy because they have no idea how he came to...you know..."

"How's Terry taking it?" Micah asked.

"It's hard to say. Teenagers eh. He doesn't say two words together and if he does one of those is usually a word I wouldn't repeat. He's away to the pub now, I hope he doesn't..."

She left the sentence unfinished.

We chatted for a while about this and that. She seemed to want the distraction. Then she surprised us by saying, 'Would you mind dropping in on Tony for a minute, he likes to have visitors."

It took me a moment to recall Tony's father, Tony senior.

"He's a bit deaf, you know but I suggest you raise your voices a bit."

Nothing could have prepared us for the sight of Tony senior. He was in the last stages of cancer and resembled a skeleton with flesh on the bones. He had a supply of oxygen cylinders. He spoke slowly, interrupting himself to breathe from a mask.

"Good of you to visit. You know if I'd known I had to do so much breathing I would never have smoked all those cigarettes."

The strange thing was that rather than us trying to make the old man feel at ease, he was very keen for us to feel comfortable in the very near presence of death.

"I'm not that bothered to be honest. The nurse comes. I'm not sure its always the same nurse. I call her Nurse Morphine. I know I could pick up heroin from (he named a local pub) but I was never sure about their quality control."

"The only trouble with morphine is that it is a bit more-ish. You don't have a cigarette about your person do you? They won't let me smoke. 'Elf and Safety' they say." He essayed a laugh but it became a cough which went on for a long time.

We went on talking. Of course he had an opinion on the government and that kept us busy for a while.

"I'd like to see them voted out but I won't live long enough, young man. Not long at all."

He was dozing when we left. We didn't wake him.

Queenie Smethwick was waiting in the lounge for us.

"You talked for a fair old while. I think he gets lonely in there. That's where Terry has been good. He goes in to talk to him. I had to stop him giving his grandad cigarettes. I am not sure what all those gas cylinders would do if there were a fire and I don't want to find out. Would you fancy a cup of tea? I know Barker would like a gravy bone, wouldn't you, boy?"

We settled down to a cup of tea on the chintz sofa and Queenie fussed over Barker. He didn't mind.

I asked a question which had been bothering me, "The NHS only supply one oxygen cylinder at a time but your father-in-law had three."

"That was my Tony that was. He knew his dad feared running out of oxygen so be bought some on Ebay. You can get all sorts on there. He was always thoughtful like that."

"Tony Senior is not long for this world. That is why he was living with us."

"One final piece," Micah said in the car on the way home and she wasn't talking about the excellent seed-cake Queenie had insisted on us taking with us.

"You got an email from the good Councillor when we had that business with our lousy neighbours. I need that and I think I can make a guess at his password. He had the word 'elephants' on the notice board by his computer."

She was on Ebay impersonating Councillor Smethwick within a minute.

"You see," she pointed to his record of purchases and she incongruously started humming "Oklahoma."

As Queenie had said, the good councillor had purchased oxygen but that was not all.

I decided to look in on young Terry in the pub.

"'Ere what do you want, grandad?" was the unpromising start. His friends thought it was hilarious though.

"I just wanted to offer my condolences on the death of your father. The councillor did the best for everyone who came to him. Is there anything I can do?"

"You can buzz off,"

"I am not sure that would be in your best interests."

"What do you mean, grandad?" his friends laughed again.

"Actually," I said so that only he could hear, "it is about your grandad that I want to talk. I saw him today."

"What about him?" he replied loudly but there was a trace of caution in his approach.

"I saw the cylinders."

Terry didn't exactly sober up but he decided he would "talk to this old geezer" and catch up with his friends later.

"Tony senior couldn't have done what he did without help."

"And what exactly do you think he did, Sherlock Holmes?"

"I'd lose the attitude if I were you," I said. All those years of teaching finally paid off. Terry sat very still.

"About the cylinders. They all have numbers on the side and are clearly labelled 'Oxygen' but there was one C259032 which wasn't. It was nitrogen."

"I didn't realise what was going to happen."

"A good solicitor would make use of that," I began.

"You don't understand. My father wanted grandad to have a peaceful death. He planned on hooking up the nitrogen cylinder while grandad was asleep – and that is a lot of the time now – and the old man would just peacefully expire. Trouble is, grandad isn't as green as he is cabbage-looking. He got to know just by reading the cylinder, there was something wrong about it. He connected it up to the defunct gas pipe that feeds the gas mantle in the lounge."

"Excuse me?"

Terry took a breath.

"He had a bit of help," he said quietly.

"From you?"

Terry nodded.

"And the dog?"

"Why do you care about the dog? A man died. I didn't realise it would kill him, I swear."

"About the dog?" I asked.

"I was the only person involved. One nitrogen cylinder and one tough plastic bag. It was a peaceful death."

"Terry, you have no idea what you did to the owners."

"Old Bolton had it coming,"

I stared him down. In the end he stared crying into his beer.

"Just one thing. Grandad isn't going to live for long. Can you hold off reporting this to the police until then?" He was pleading and I was touched.

"And can you volunteer for the Dogs Trust?" I asked.

We shook hands on it.

I reported back to Micah.

"So you got the Oklahoma connection?" she asked.

"I can use Google too, you know. Oklahoma uses nitrogen gas for executions."

"We can't leave it too long to report this," she said.

"We won't have to," I spoke with more certainty than I felt but I was proved right within a fortnight. I don't know if they could have arrested Tony senior, they certainly couldn't have brought him to trial. As it was, Terry got a reduced sentence as an accessory because he was 'acting under the instructions of his grandfather.'

# Where there's a will there's a relative

The death of Jay Ericson was not strange or paradoxical or suspicious. He had a long history of heart disease with three rather long stays in Worthing hospital. Medical science had done all it could for him and the doctor's certificate recorded 'myocardial infarction' as the cause of death.

"Have you ever met him?" Micah asked on the way home from church.

"I may have attended a service with him but, no we didn't talk."

"I remember him as a name on the list of the sick of the parish before he was bumped up to the list of recently deceased. Sekonda rang this afternoon while you were out."

"Sekonda? He wasn't..."

"Hm yes he was one of those who made use of her perfectly respectable escort service from time to time. Apparently, well I won't dwell on the medical details. Suffice to say that his partner Edgar Marinson was not aware."

"But the death?"

"Nothing suspicious about it, according to Sekonda. What is suspicious is the will. Edgar Marinson is furious about it."

"Why?"

"Jay, whose full name was Johannes Ericson, had been with Edgar for ten years. He has an estranged wife, she reverted to her maiden name, Pauline Spenser. His son and daughter also took her name, that's Paula Spenser and Pavel Spenser."

"I take it Edgar didn't get what he was expecting."

"He got a thousand pounds. The remainder of the estate, £500,000 or thereabouts, was all left to young Pavel. Pavel has not seen his father for ten years and claims to be as mystified as everybody else."

"If it was that mysterious he didn't have a motive of any kind and it is not clear that a crime has been committed," I said.

Micah agreed. "That is why Sekonda contacted us instead of the police. Edgar hasn't the money to afford a solicitor to contest the will but it would probably do no harm to find out more details."

"I will pop round to see Sekonda," I said.

"Correction, **we** will go round to see Sekonda," Micah said.

"I know exactly what you want and I've got it right here for you," Sekonda always knew the way to Barker's heart and produced a series of Bakers' Allsorts treats during the visit.

"I guess this is about poor old Jay. My clients never give me their names of course but I usually know somebody who knows somebody so I knew all about Jay, his ex wife and children and current partner. I gave all this to Micah..." she said.

Micah nodded and produced her old-fashioned notebook as if to prove it.

Sekonda's flat in Broadwater belied its surroundings. The furnishings could be described as sumptuous and as close to those of Kensington Palace as was possible. I used to teach Sekonda when he/she went by the name of George Whyte before she reinvented herself using the name of her watch as a soubriquet. I hadn't predicted what George's career path would be.

"The death, Craig, was not suspicious as such. Jay once gave me a list of his heart medication and it took up most of his session. He didn't seem to mind. The death was certified by a competent doctor whose father I... er happen to know...a Doctor Smart. The old windbag Doctor Winter has been persuaded to resign. He was past retirement age anyway."

"Dr Smart did all the proper toxicology tests. Jay was not poisoned and his levels of the medication he normally took were all within proper parameters. The only thing he would say is that a heart attack can be brought on by stress even if the heart condition itself has a different genesis. The post-mortem could not confirm or deny that."

"However, Micah, I want you to find out what the police know. They are not officially interested in the case but Edgar, as they say, "has form" by which they mean that as a teenager he was cautioned for taking and driving away his father's car. The offence was 'spent' but somehow they still had the records."

"I believe that the heir to Jay had not seen him for at least ten years but you might like to check on that. The will was incomprehensible but in your hands it will not remain so for long."

"Now what can I do for you?" Sekonda added.

"It's a lot to ask, Sekonda, but can you let us have a list of the clients whose identity you know? I imagine that's all of them."

"Most," Sekonda smiled, "I will want the list destroyed when this investigation is over."

"Of course."

"I can get them to you by email this afternoon. Now about payment?"

I was about to say something about 'mates' rates' when Micah produced a scale of charges she always carried around.

She added, "Of course there will be a discount for all the cases you've helped us with."

Sekonda smiled.

Over a cup of tea, Micah composed a list

- Pauline - Why estranged?
- Paula – did she keep in touch? How did she feel about Pavel getting the cash?
- Pavel – did he split the money with Paula and Pauline? Has he a theory as to why Jay made him his heir? Had they really not met for ten years?

- Edgar Marinson – if he knew about the will it was a motive. If he knew about Sekonda it was another motive.

- The 60000 dollar question: was it really natural causes or something else?

"Jay was an electrician before he retired and at that time he advertised in the local paper. Very usefully he had a website and an email address linked to the website. My bet is that he went on using it."

"So it's just a matter of getting his password," I said.

It was Micah's turn to smile.

Trawling through the emails, looking for something fishy was a long job. I took Barker for a walk and started work on the steak and ale pie. Ideally I should have started work on it the day before but the fact remains that I didn't.

I looked up when Micah came into the kitchen.

"PGP," she said.

"Oh," I said.

"Oh indeed. Most of the emails were routine. I did learn why Pauline left him. It wasn't anything to do with his sexuality. Apparently he was making a lot of money and the more that he made, the more tight-fisted he became.

"There are a number of emails from her about financial matters and although they were never divorced she did manage to get some kind of settlement out of him. It could not be described as generous and that was not one of the words Pauline used to describe it either."

"However he made use of PGP encryption which the CIA claim they cannot break. Neither can I, unfortunately. There is one email address in particular. It was "kismet88@gmail.com" and all of the traffic associated with it was encrypted. It tells us something of course. He and his email correspondent had something to hide, what it doesn't tell us is precisely what."

"What is our next move?"

"Condolences to Edgar. I'll handle that. Which pub does Pavel drink in? Which library does he use? Cafes, shops, all the places you could bump into him would be worth a look, Craig. Then we can compare notes. Anyway that's for tomorrow. As for tonight, are there any horrible murders on ITV3?"

There were three.

It was easy enough to track down Pavel. He was very popular in both of his local pubs, whether this came after his good fortune I can only speculate. He had chucked in his job with the council and was spending like a sailor, or Macheath perhaps.

I tried to buy a drink but he would have none of it. He insisted on buying one for me . I offered my condolences on the death of his father but he would have none of that either.

"I didn't know him. I hadn't seen him for years. Why did he leave me the money? I don't know. He might have felt guilty about doing the dirty on his family but he did leave it a bit late to show it. Have another drink? Oh you're OK are you? Bit of a lightweight, eh?"

He was a young man. I estimated he was in his early twenties. Paula was still in school. Pauline worked for the council. She was in the same department as Pavel and quite possibly she was the reason he had the job he had just quit.

"How's your mum feel about you leaving your job?"

"You're very nosy. Isn't he nosy?"

"I'm just interested. I suppose it's quite a big issue to leave a good job."

"Well I'll tell you what. It's quite a big issue to get half a million quid out of the blue."

His friends, apparently most of the people in the bar, raised a cheer at that.

"And anyway it was a rubbish job really," he confided. "Paula is just a kid but I'll see that mum is all right for cash. She was a one-parent family, you know."

"Yes, I understand you were a one-parent family. It must have been hard."

"Well that shows how much you know. She had one of those things. Help me out here."

"A divorce settlement?" I suggested.

"No no no. She was never, you know wassisnamed. Divorced in fact. No but he did give her some money in the end. He was a complete skinflint but the court, you see, the court they. What did they do?"

"Insisted he support his children?"

"The court insisted, yes. Do you want another drink, Mr Lightweight?"

Micah immediately highlighted the most important fact as soon as I told her about this. Her visit to Mr Marinson had not gone particularly well.

"I've come to offer you my condolences, Mr Marinson."

"Why?"

"Condolences on the death of..."

"Oh shut up. Don't treat me like an idiot. Have you got a tape recorder?"

"No," she said accurately. She records these things on her phone.

"I have nothing to say to you. Now good day. You can take your condolences and..."

She didn't record his interesting suggestion on that point.

"So now we have a talk with Pauline and Paula?"

"That would be good. Then I will be making use of the information you got."

Sekonda emailed us a detailed list of her clients. It was a bit too detailed in some places and I think she was trying to shock. I think many residents of Worthing would be surprised to see who was on her little list but of course this story is not about that. One name leapt out because he had been in the pub when I met Pavel. I made a note to talk to him when we had finished with Pauline and her daughter.

Micah showed her realisitic Press Card (which mainly impresses people who have not seen a real one).

"This is my photographer. I would like to talk to you about the death of Jay Ericson and your side of the story of the unexpected windfall your son received in his will."

"In the first place, his name was Johannes and I think you should get that right. In the second place, I suggest you go away and look up the word "estranged" because I have nothing further to say to you. Print what you like."

"But..."

And she shut the door.

Micah shrugged.

I will visit an Anglican church in the line of duty. They protest that they believe in one holy catholic and apostolic church. Some do. Some don't.

It was one of those days of sunshine and high winds for which Worthing is noted. I caught up with one of Sekonda's clients, a Dave Porter, in the car park of St Symphorian's.

"Sad about Jay Ericson, isn't it?"

"I suppose so. Mind you, he didn't look too bright on the occasions on which I saw him, trouble breathing and what have you. I didn't know him very well. I knew his son, Pavel rather better. We had, shall I say, different lifestyles."

"You had a friend in common though. Sekonda."

Mr Porter looked a bit nonplussed for a moment, then he guffawed.

"Why the old dog! Full of surprises he was."

"Well he left his money to a son he hadn't seen for ten years."

"Get away. Mind you he had seen Pavel more recently."

I paused.

He continued, "It was in the library. It was, let me think, during the last series of *Game of Thrones.* I remember because I was there to get the book. They didn't talk much. Jay gave a large envelope to Pavel and Pavel said something. He used the word 'renege.' I was surprised because it did not seem the sort of word Pavel would know."

I thought I had done well so I went back to give Micah the good news. She wrote it down but I could tell she had some news for me. It seems that one bit of information from my chat with Pavel had borne fruit. I had mentioned the school Paula was attending. Micah knew in the way she tended to know these things that the main problem with pupils having email accounts was that they lost their passwords with monotonous regularity.

The school had come up with a solution of sorts. The school website had a "secret room" where pupils could give their email address and get their password. Of course they might as well have left the door of the "secret room" open for all the good it did against Micah's dark arts.

"Pavel you see was a good big brother. He wanted to bring his little sister up to speed with his computer skills. So he had done the unthinkable and given the private key to his PGP cypher to her by email. This means that none of the encrypted emails were encypted any more. I have printed off two relevant ones."

Micah handed the emails to me.

It didn't take me long to decide. We should first confront Pavel with the emails, then forward the information to Sekonda and then contact the police.

We arranged to meet Pavel in the Black Cat.

"You were blackmailing your father."

I expected protestations of innocence but Pavel got up to leave.

"You can go of course but don't you want to know how we know?"

Pavel sat down.

Micah passed the first email across the table.

"Where did you get this?"

"You can deny that this is your email but you cannot deny you became the beneficiary of your father's estate because you threatened to expose his relationship with Sekonda. It does not matter whether you admit the murder."

"What murder?"

"Your father died from a myocardial infarction. How much stress do you think being blackmailed by his own son caused?"

Pavel got up again.

Micah just produced the second email.

Pavel returned to the table. He looked at the email but he didn't need to read it.

"It says, 'I have always hated you and the sooner you are dead, the sooner your family can move on. You are a skinflint and a philanderer. Any sign of you reneging by trying to write another will and I will use social media – if you even know what that is – so everybody knows exactly what you are like. Just go away and die.' "

"We are handing all this information over to Sekonda and to the police," Micah concluded, "you may go."

When Pavel arrived home, the police were already there.

Pavel went to jail for blackmail. The judge concluded that the blackmail had 'probably' shortened Jay's life but the evidence was inconclusive.

Jay's money went into the pockets of the lawyers as his two families disputed the will.

# Death by Python

It began with one of Micah's infernal guessing games. The clue was the headline from the *Worthing Herald*, MAN SLAIN BY PYTHON. She covered over the rest of the story and the telling picture. Apart from the uncharacteristic verb "slain" there were no clues.

"A surviving member of Monty Python decided the bump off someone who didn't share their sense of humour?"

"Ingenious, Craig. Wrong though. You have two more guesses. And don't sigh. Sighs ain't everything."

"I've seen someone walking around with a python draped round their neck. Maybe the python started to crush them while crossing the road and a passing car finished them off."

I could tell from Micah's expression that this wasn't right.

"OK last guess. He was possessed by his own personal demon which was a python and took his own life."

"You're getting better at this. Still quite off the beam but quite clever."

She handed the paper to me then snatched it back.

"After you buy me a drink."

When I returned from the bar, I read, "Police were baffled as to how Mr Rod Vickers had been killed in a locked factory on Tuesday of last week. The body of Mr Vickers was found by his live-in girlfriend Sheil Pollard when he didn't come home."

"'He's been out on a bender once in a while so I thought nothing of it. But then the time went on and I became worried. I have keys to the factory because I work there and Rod trusts me...trusted me... with them. I can't believe he's dead. At first I thought it was one of his jokes but when I found the bolt had gone through the back of his head I had to think again,' she said."

"Mr Vickers had been shot through the head by a bolt gun which was controlled by a computer program. The program was written in Python which Mr Vickers was known to use. To all intents and purposes he had taken his own life in a mysterious way. However the police are treating the death as suspicious when it was revealed that Mr Vickers had received death threats in the recent past."

"Inspector Tillotson appealed to anyone who was in the vicinity of Vickers' Workshop last Monday or Tuesday so they can be eliminated from the inquiry."

By this time, Micah had googled Vickers on her phone and made a list of the employees of the small workshop. She wrote them down in the notebook she always carried.

- Rod Vickers
- Sheil Pollard
- Cor Norfield
- Shay Cambury
- Car Waters

She added "Check if Vickers Australian."

To me she said, "I noticed none of them can spare more than a syllable in the first name. New South Wales is awash with abbreves."

"A bolt gun?"

"There is a loophole in the law which means that this lethal device is not classified as a firearm. It is usually used to slaughter animals. However we should look into why Vickers owned one when his day-to-day business was light engineering not cattle slaughtering."

"We want to know why they had one. And what was the nature of the threats which had been made."

It was at this point that a text message came through on Micah's phone. Only old Ben Tillotson always texted in block capitals. It was as if he were shouting. "CONTACT ME ASAP RE VICKERY SLAYING".

Micah texted back that we would meet him in the John Selden. "I MEANT JUST YOU BUT YOU MAY AS WELL BOTH COME" was the charming response.

The John Selden is a most soothing place and even old Ben seems half way human when we meet him there. He was accompanied by a female police expert in her mid-twenties called Joanne Thallman. He introduced her as "My Q". When she looked a question at him, he went into a laboured exegisis of the Bond film reference.

"Well that's an improvement," said Micah, "he usually calls technical experts 'boffins'."

"Oh believe me, he does that too," said Joanne.

Old Ben sat back with his pint of Harveys and let Sergeant Joanne Thallman do the talking.

"As you know, any sane person who is writing a computer program will 'comment out' making clear what the different parts of the program mean. Without the comments it is a bit of a nightmare. And I fear, Micah, your task should you choose to accept it is to go through the nightmare and tell us everything you can find out about it."

"You will of course be paid for your time and as a civilian expert seconded to the police force the rate of pay is in the region of bugger-all."

Old Ben looked as though he was going to disagree but then realised it was nothing but the truth. He added, "We will of course take the pair of you on as experts but the pay will still be in the same region for two."

"I'm always happy to help the police but surely you have your own experts."

"All tied up and in any case their area of expertise is not Python," said Joanne, "the bolt gun was not in itself illegal but we strongly suspect that the program was. The bolt gun was so positioned and programmed that it would deter anyone who tried to burgle the premises. As far as we can tell it would be inoperative if there were any members of staff present but any interlopers would be seriously injured or killed. It would have been hard to gloss over it as an accident but Mr Vickers had his own way of going about things."

"Was he Australian?"

"Yes. Homicidal factory owners are not commonplace in Australia, so how did you know?"

"The brevity of the names of the employees was a hint," said Micah.

"I will email the program code to you in the next five minutes and if you could get to work as soon as poss, that would be appreciated."

As good as her word, Joanne sent the code from her smart phone to Micah's laptop before we left the pub.

"I had a little peek at old Ben's computer, now we are working officially with the police it is practically legal. All of the employees claim to have no knowledge of Python. Either one or more of them is fibbing or Vickers was a victim of his own incompetence. I will be up until the early hours with this malarkey but I am sure someone can make me a pot of ridiculously strong coffee."

"It's the least I can do," I said.

"Yes it is," Micah smiled.

Micah came to bed at 3 am, remarking, 'Tell you in the morning," before falling into a deep sleep. In the morning she was more communicative after downing a couple of cups of tea.

"Any computer progam, even the Basic you used to use, needs comments. You can include them in the code with the right punctuation. If you don't want anyone else to understand it you could just leave the comments out of the final version of the code. What this code does is complex.

"If there are staff on the premises there is a section of the code which will ensure the bolt gun will not fire. If there are people on the premises it triggers sensors. A proximity sensor will fire the gun very precisely if someone is in range. It would be the same if it were a cat or a rat. Then there is a whole block of code I couldn't understand at first until I realised it was using facial recognition software to identify precisely which member of staff was on the premises and keep a record of who was in when. We should be able to access that log. I will arrange for Joanne to send over the computer itself later today or we can visit the police station to have a look if that is what they prefer. I have to go through this rigmarole because this particular computer was never connected to the internet."

"However, the key fact is that there is a simple line of code which bypasses the subroutine which prevents the gun firing. Again the pattern recognition software is used but one face in particular is not recognised. We can probably guess which one. That person would then be treated like an intruder after a time lapse of 25 seconds."

Joanne not only sent over the computer but two badges which had our photos and the word "Police" in large letters and an explanation that we were not police officers in smaller letters. We somehow managed to forget to return them when the case was over. Micah looked at the computer in much the same way that a child regards a Christmas stocking. I left her to her delights.

My first interview of the day was with Sheil Pollard, the 28-year-old girlfriend of Rod Vickers (54).

"We are investigating the computer system in the workshop, can you help us at all?"

"Well, (she read my badge) Craig, I don't think so. I don't know anything about it. If you want my opinion, Vic (he liked us to call him 'Vic') was killed by that awful bolt gun because he was rocking back in his chair. I've told him about it a thousand times."

"I see. Do you know anything about Python?"

"A python? In here? You're having a laugh aren't you. We've had some odd things in here, clocks, bicycles and once a snooker table but no pythons. Not even one."

"Methinks the lady doth protest too much," Micah commented when I phoned her, explaining, "She sends emails on her phone and uses WhatsApp and Google. The more she denies knowing anything, the more suspicious we should be."

I didn't have to ask how Micah knew these details.

The next interview was with Col Norfield. He was a teenager and the latest employee in the workshop. I caught the way he was looking at Sheil. So did she and met it with a frown. I wasn't going to mention the issue but he was.

"He's too old for 'er. I mean he was but he's brown bread now isn't he?"

"That's what I wanted to talk about, Col. How much do you know about the security system here?"

Col laughed. "I know anybody who broke in was in for a nasty surprise. Of course the whys and wherefores of how it worked I couldn't tell you."

"Did you do any computer programming at school?"

"I ain't at school nah. Listen, Mister, I know my rights. I'll get my solicitor in here if you're asking questions."

"'My solicitor' are the two most expensive words in the English language, Col. It was a fairly straightforward question,"I said.

"Well I'm giving you a straightforward answer. No."

"No you didn't do any computer programming?"

"No I ain't answering your question."

"Do you like working here?"

Col folded his arms and repeated something he probably heard on the TV, "No comment."

And that was that. He'd already given away the most important fact and his school record wouldn't exactly tax Micah's investigative prowess.

Shay Cambury was in his early twenties. He was dismissive of Col's bravado.

"I'll answer any question you have for me, officer."

I didn't tell him I was an officer, but I wasn't denying it either.

"We are investigating the computer fault which caused Mr Vickers' death. Do you know anything about the system?"

"Of course," he looked over at Col who was sitting in the corner and having a sulk, "everybody does computer science at school these days. Those who have the brains probably remember some of it too. I am not going to pretend to know the details of the programming. Python was a bit above my pay grade if you know what I mean. I knew it was a system designed to deter intruders. Vic, that's Mr Vickers, said he set it up after some young tearaways," (he couldn't resist looking across at Col as an example when he said it) " broke in and wrecked a thousand quid's worth of gear."

"Was it legal to set up such a lethal system?"

"I would imagine it wasn't but I didn't set it up. It was all Vic and Sheil," he gave a sly grin as Sheil bridled, "Sorry, I mean it was all Vic of course."

We talked for a while about the set-up at the workshop and who was responsible for what. I noticed the way he looked at Sheil and she didn't frown. If anything she seemed rather in awe of Shay. He was careful not to mention anyone else in relation to the lethal computer.

Des Lovelace was in his mid-forties and was the senior member of staff after Mr Vickers.

"I were responsible for all the work in the factory, materials, tools, wages, outgoings and so forth."

"Computers?"

"Well I were responsible but you can hardly expect an old fogey like me to know much about them. I just plug them in and run the spreadsheets."

"Who does the website?"

"Website, lad? Website? There's a spider over in the corner, that's the only web around here. We get on with word of mouth around these parts. Website indeed."

He didn't look at Shirl. I noticed he didn't look in her general direction either.

Car Waters was in her mid-thirties. She seemed genuinely affected by Mr Vickers' death.

"It was terrible about Mr Vickers and I know our Shirl was really cut up about it, weren't you, dear? He was always rocking back on that chair. The number of times I've thought of telling him it was dangerous so close to that awful bolt gun thing but it really wasn't my place. Shirl and I did talk about it and I know she was worried too."

"Look, is this going to take long? I've got a lot of work on and with Mr Vickers, well with the, you know how it is. We have to keep working you see."

"Who takes over the workshop now?"

"I really think I should get back to work, Mr McLairy."

"Are you going to take all morning with this, Craig?" asked Sheil, "The fact is that I take over the workshop now and I want Car to get back to work."

"Just one question then, did you know anything about the computer system?"

"I know I'd throw it in the sea if I could. What a terrible thing to do. I know nothing about them of course. You need brains for that kind of malarkey and I'm just one of the hands."

I had recorded all this on the phone and Micah and I discussed it. Micah also had the log of staff attendance at the workshop.

"The log is not as useful as it might be. There is no record of anyone being in the workshop alone. As a rule Mr Vickers would turn up with the keys and let them all in at 8.30 am. They all left for a lunch break from 12 to 1 and the only person who ever stayed after 5 was the murder victim."

"The staff ignorance of Python was backed up by their computer ownership. They all had phones of course but I wouldn't like to try writing a complex program on a phone. Only Shay had a laptop and police confirm that he only used it for gaming and porn. There are no erased files of python code."

"However," Micah can do the dramatic pause to perfection, "they didn't need to."

"You mean..."

"Give me a minute and I will tell you what I mean. In the erased file area on the workshop computer there was a small program which would over-ride the main program and make exactly the changes we found. It is an off-the-shelf module. Anybody could have used it without knowing anything about Python. They just needed to know how to insert a memory stick to upload the program. The work of five minutes. Is it possible to do that without anyone else in the workshop seeing you do it?"

I sat down and made a diagram. I did this as much to revive my own memory as to show Micah.

"Very risky but possible. More so if the killer had an accomplice to divert attention from what they were doing. It must have been done on the day Mr Vickers died," I said.

"There was no copy of the original program with comments anywhere so I can only assume the comments were stripped out of the code once it had been tested."

"I have been doing a bit of research. To be precise the police and my friend Google have done most of the work of course."

"Rod Vickers was not a nice man. Sheil has been described as his girlfriend but in fact she only got the job on condition of taking on that role. She was desperate for work. By all accounts, by which I mean mainly Col, Shay and Car, he treated her appallingly. He was not actually violent but he was exceptionally unpleasant when drunk and that was most nights."

"I am interested that Des didn't have a word to say against Mr Vickers. He repeated that he had given them all jobs as if it were philanthropy on his part. Did you get the impression that they were all a bit in love with Sheil?"

"Except Des."

"Interesting that. Well it is a possible motive. However the person with most easy access to the computer was Des. I have had a look at his spreadsheets. They are protected of course but there is a little app you can use to look at them. The business was ticking over as far as I can see and there was no evidence that anyone had a hand in the till."

"Except of course that Des was in the best position to cover up any such thing," I said.

Micah nodded.

"The threat to Mr Vickers was reported to the police by Sheil on the day of the murder. She said that Mr Vickers had had a threatening phone call on their home phone. She knew nothing more about it than that. There were calls to that number from unknown cell phone numbers but nothing that could be traced. The threat could have been irrelevant. The caller didn't actually threaten to kill him but made it clear they disliked him intensely. Mr Vickers didn't recognise the voice."

"And the whole thing could have been made up by Sheil," I said.

Micah nodded.

The next morning, Micah was on her laptop after breakfast. There was nothing unusual about that. What was unusual was that she silently handed it over to me. It was the *Worthing Herald* Website.

"Police were called to the home of the late Rod Vickers whose death we reported last week. Rod's girlfriend, Sheila Pollard, had failed to turn up for work and police had taken the decision to break down the door. Ms Pollard was found drowned in the bath. The police have not ruled out foul play."

"Forensic pathologist, Dr Swift, will be carrying out a post-mortem in the next twenty four hours."

"Thank God it's Swift."

"Winter's dead," Micah remarked.

"I didn't kill him."

"So you say."

Micah's text alert went off.

"I'VE GOT A LITTLE SOMETHING FOR YOU. I WILL SEND IT ROUND POST-HASTE. PLEASE GIVE SERGEANT THALLMAN ALL THE GEN ASAP."

Inspector Tillotson was as good as his word and the front door bell rang within the hour. Sergeant Joanne Thallman seemed flustered. We sat her down and offered her a cup of tea.

"What have you brought me?" Micah asked.

For answer, Joanne handed over a memory stick.

"Where did this come from?"

"I'm not supposed to tell you."

"But you will," Micah said confidently.

Joanne hesitated.

"I can tell you today is the first time I've seen a dead body. I can't wait to get off duty and get myself outside a glass of Cab Sav. I can't tell you where the memory stick came from."

"And you haven't," Micah played along.

Joanne had another cup of tea while Micah plugged the memory stick in to her laptop. The room went silent.

Micah put a second memory stick into the computer. She was knocking seven bells out of the keyboard for a good fifteen minutes. She looked up at Joanne and said one word, "Yes."

Joanne relaxed.

Micah continued, "This is either the original or a copy of the one used to upload the  program used to kill Mr Vickers. The program has been erased but the memory stick has not been reformatted. I don't need to tell you that I can use an app to unerase the file and it is identical to the one which was erased from the workshop desktop. Has it been fingerprinted?"

"It was wiped."

"You will have worked out that Ms Pollard could not have put the program on to this memory stick, not at home anyway." Micah said.

"We think she may have used a computer in the library. In theory people have to produce a card to use a library computer but in practice all they have to produce is a number and that could come from any card. We have checked that none of the other employees were indicated as having used the library computer system in Worthing."

"You will have checked whether Mr Vickers used the system," said Micah.

Joanne looked crestfallen. She compensated by explaining to Micah how to hack into the library computer system. I think Joanne must have been blessed with a grandmother who did not know how to suck eggs.

In five minutes, Micah had the answer. Mr Vickers had been using the computer system in the large Worthing central library. She cross-referenced the times with the employee log.

"It seems he had the power to be in two places at once," Micah said.

Joanne smiled for the first time.

"So the prime projection is that one of the employees was forging the instrument of his death while using his library number."

"'Prime projection'? Are you a fan of Frank Herbert?"

"How about substituting 'It is likely' for 'The prime projection is'? Are you a fan?"

"I read them all, my favourite is *Chapter House Dune.*"

We spent an enjoyable few minutes discussing Frank Herbert but Joanne had to get back to work. We invited her for dinner 'with a plus one'. Her plus one proved to be a detective constable called Janet Small. She looked for us to be shocked but no friend of Sekonda is shockable.

It was a chance to cook a serious penne carbonara. Joanne had already expressed a preference for Cab Sav but we put a bottle of Sauvignon Blanc in the fridge in case Janet had a different taste in wine.

"You are adorable," Janet Small was in our good books already with her greeting to Barker. She also brought a bottle of Nuit St Georges which did her reputation no harm.

We talked books and films during the meal but I knew we would discuss the case at some point in the evening.

"I've been to the library today," said Janet.

The sergeant looked at the constable but then shrugged. We might as well share information.

"They didn't remember everybody who used the computers. It is a large library. However the system could identify which computer the supposed Mr Vickers had used and there was one member of staff who remembered who had been using the computer. It was a man who had serious BO. That was the only thing she remembered about him but it was very memorable."

That was when I knew who had killed the unpleasant Mr Vickers but could we prove it?

We discussed ways and means from then on.

The findings of the post-mortem were ambiguous. There was a lot of alcohol in Sheil's bloodstream, quite enough to explain her drowning in the bath. The only thing was that one of her teeth had been broken. Dr Swift could not say that this definitely proved the alcohol had been forced into her but it was quite possible.

Constable Small took a set of photos to the library but the member of staff could not recognise any of them. She had actually not looked at the man.

Identity parades are notorious in cases of miscarriages of justice but Sergeant Thallman persuaded old Ben Tillotson that it would conclusively identify the murderer. He took pleasure in telling her that on its own it would not be enough.

I fervently hoped the suspect hadn't started using Lifebuoy Soap. I took comfort in the probability that he would be sweating even more than usual in this stressful situation.

Sure enough the librarian could identify the person who had used the computer with Mr Vickers' library number. She only had to follow her nose.

Micah sat in on the interview as a police expert with the consent of the suspect. The suspect had also consented to having a shower and a change of clothes although I don't think that part was entirely voluntary.

"You downloaded a bit of code which set off the bolt gun."

"Says who?"

"It was in a public library. You took a risk and it didn't pay off."

There was a silence into which Micah dropped "Each man kills the thing he loves." as an aside.

"*The Ballad of Reading Gaol,*" said the suspect automatically as if this were a quiz show.

Micah sat forward.

"Did Sheil turn you down?" she asked.

"I don't know what you're on about." the suspect replied.

"Did you force whisky on her?" asked Sergeant Thallman.

"It was just a game and she didn't need no forcing."

"So you admit you were there?"

"I never said I wasn't."

"If you didn't force her, how did she break her tooth?"

"I dunno. She was pretty drunk when I left."

"Did you leave because she turned you down? How did you feel about that?"

"I wasn't interested."

"Then why the drinking game?"

"Just a bit of fun."

The two women just sat and looked.

Des Lovelace let out a stream of abuse about Sheil. He brought out the obscenities mechanically as if he couldn't help himself. In the end he just started crying.

"Tell me all about it," said Sergeant Thallman.

And he did.

He had, in his words, "had his eyes on the little whore" since she started in the workshop. With Vic out of the way he was going to step into Vic's role. Sheil had just laughed at him and then "something snapped" when she said he'd have to get a good wash for starters. Then she laughed again.

"And I don't like whisky," were her final words.

"We'll see about that," he said.

He said he had only vague memories of the actual murder.

"The look in his eyes said something else," Micah remarked when at last she got home. "He did remember it and he was going to savour it for all those long years in prison. Perhaps his inner demon was a python after all. They can be quite nasty."

# Voodoo Doll

I knew Zac Moyes. He was a Eucharistic Minister, which means he administers the Eucharist if that's clear. He was also a Catholic Justice and Peace co-ordinator and, as far as I knew, an all-round good person. It was a double shock, therefore, when Micah discovered on social media that he had died from a heart attack and that the internet was awash with images of a voodoo doll with a tiny stake through the heart which the police had dug up in his garden.

The police don't normally go in for gardening so we assumed that they were treating his death as suspicious. Micah soon got the reason for the suspicion from browsing Inspector Ben Tillotson's laptop remotely.

"There was an anonymous tip-off that there was a voodoo doll buried in the garden. It didn't give any more details. Mind you it is very difficult to be anonymous these days. Phones and email are monitored, handwritten or typed notes are subject to all sorts of tests to prove their origin. This anonymous person knew their business. They used a spoof IP address to send a message to Sergeant Joanne Thallman's twitter account and she passed it on to old Ben."

"I doubt if old Ben knows what a twitter account is," I ventured to suggest.

"Neither do you," Micah responded.

I was interested enough to ask Sekonda about voodoo dolls. She laughed.

"I think you need to talk to Yolanda, she is the expert on Voodoo in these parts but be careful, Craig, she is a very clever woman."

Sekonda had her address. She is a mine of information.

Yolanda turned out to be a charming pensioner who welcomed me into her home. I cannot recommend her tea however.

"I am from the *Worthing Journal*," I showed her my fake press card.

"Tell me, how is your brother getting on?" She asked.

She bustled about making tea for us.

"He's very well, thank you," I said eventually.

"Quite over his illness then?"

"Yes, how did you know..."

"Craig McLairy, don't take me for a fool. I know about you and your detective agency. I know you've come to talk to me about voodoo dolls. I know your brother had a serious abdominal illness and was in hospital for a week. I'm pleased he is on the mend by the way."

"Now show me these pictures and no more lies please."

I showed her the pictures of the voodoo doll which had been on twitter and facebook.

"And this was found buried in the garden of poor Mr Moyes?"

"Yes."

"He was a fine man. A man with no prejudices, Mr McLairy. I can bet you a hundred pounds he wouldn't have believed in voodoo dolls for a single minute and I'll tell you why. Voodoo dolls only exist in fiction. They are in books and films the white supremacists used to raise up hatred against people like me."

She grinned. I can't recommend her dentist either.

"They don't like people of colour and they hate women in particular. The poppet was a figure in folklore in Europe long before there was such a thing as Louisiana or the enslavement of Africa. A doll was baptised with the name of the person they wanted to harm. Anything done to the poppet would happen to the person it represented."

She continued, "Voodoo is about keeping in touch with the spirits of our ancestors. What you believe is not that different."

"You must understand that the person who told the police about the doll must be the person who put it there. And Mr Moyes wasn't frightened to death nor is it a case of natural causes either."

"You see, I could be a detective too," she added.

"Will you help us?" I found myself asking.

"I've been helping you. If there is anything else I can do for you just tell me. Pray for me, Mr McLairy and I will pray for you."

I told Micah that I wasn't sure what to make of all this.

"Whatever I'd been drinking it wasn't tea."

"What do you mean?"

"I had the feeling if I'd stayed much longer I'd have agreed with anything Yolanda Moughan had to say. I might even have signed up to the voodoo religion."

"I imagine Father Simon would have been less than pleased about that," Micah smiled, then she was all businesslike again.

"I think you established quite a lot. The doll was intended to implicate Yolanda Moughan or her co-religionists. I agree with her that the planter of the doll and the murderer could well be one and the same person. I haven't been idle while you've been away. Let's take Barker for a walk and I can tell you all about it."

"I'm not paranoid," she said, looking around suspiciously at the trees in Pond Lane Recreation Ground as if they might be listening in.

"However, I am not in favour of saying anything about this in the house. The local police have acquired a new recruit. A PC called Alan Stubbins has joined them and he has a lot of seniority for a new recruit. There is a cryptic comment about him on the file which indicated that he 'went dark' for a number of years. I don't think that means he went over to the First Order, Craig. I think it means something else but I am not sure. He is being restricted to station duties and kept away from the general public."

Micah was seldom unsure.

"It is an offence, I believe it is a terrorist offence in fact, to take a photograph of a police officer. However, I printed this out from his file. Be careful who you show it to."

"To whom I show it," I couldn't resist.

"I'm glad you've got the important point of the case in the front of your mind," Micah can be sarky at times.

"There were a number of files linked to the death of Zac which relate to the local Justice and Peace activists. The police were extraordinarily interested in them. Justice and Peace opposed the policy of creating a hostile environment for migrants. They thought it meant unleashing hatred against the migrant community. The police files are extremely detailed."

"I think we will pay a visit to Milly, I haven't seen her in years. We'll take Barker, she always spoils him rotten."

Micah smiled and nodded.

Magda "Milly" Vail wasn't an official member of any group but if there were any railings to handcuff herself to, she was always the one to do it.

When she had loaded us up with cakes and Gravybones for Barker and poured a couple of generous Sangiovese, she pledged us to write to our 'useless article of an MP' (her words) and to think about joining a march in Brighton against racism.

Then she relaxed.

"I think you might know this person, it's not a very good picture."

Micah handed over the picture. It was a grainy black and white likeness but Milly recognised it at once.

"Oh yes," she said enthusiatically (although enthusiastic is a default mode for Milly), "that's young Byron, just a minute, yes Byron Marcel. It was a double blow, Zac dying and Byron disappearing in the same week. Anti-racists are thin on the ground in Worthing. A bit like hens' teeth if I can mix a metaphor."

"Byron was what you might call an activist. He had all sorts of contacts in Brighton and Worthing and he was always urging people to do more for the cause even if it meant breaking the law."

"If you are investigating Zac's death, the three of you ought to look into Byron's disappearance as well."

"Oh, we will," we promised.

Back home, drinking tea and relaxing on a disreputable sofa, Micah was reflective.

"I think it's only on ITV3 that police officers, even undercover ones, go around committing murder. The aim of the game is to get radicals of any sort to commit criminal acts so they can be arrested. The French invented the idea and the term 'agent provocateur' in the early 19th Century."said Micah.

"And there was I thinking they were a lingerie retailer."

"Not helpful, Craig."

"What Milly said squares with that. We still need to know why he came in from the cold though. More to the point why he did so in the same week Zac was found dead. Any news on the post mortem?" I asked.

Micah pulled out her laptop and within minutes she had cracked the pathetic security of old Ben Tillotson's laptop.

"Zac was not a regular cocaine user so Doctor Swift concluded that the presence of cocaine in his bloodstream was connected with the cardiac arrest ('heart attack' she added for my benefit). It looked very much as though as a first time user, Zac had overdosed accidentally. It will probably be recorded as 'death by misadventure' although no doubt the press will continue the 'voodoo curse' story because it is more colourful."

In that she was wrong. Although the local papers made use of the voodoo curse story it was only in order to debunk it. The nationals, most notably the Daily Mail, were more interested in the 'Leftist cocaine overdose' angle.

The article in the *Worthing Herald* was accompanied with tributes from friends and foes. Zac's opponents said that he was "committed and extreme in his views but fair minded' and a 'humane and thoughtful man despite his cranky opinions'. Micah noted down the names although they could hardly be regarded as suspects.

"We can hardly make a note of every racist in Worthing, I'd run out of notebooks."

The police house-to-house inquiries were wound up after the post mortem. However we decided to do some of our own focussing on the burial of the doll. A witness who had seen the act was unlikely ('impossible' was Micah's analysis) but any strangers would be noticed in Zac's street or so we hoped.

"I think we can narrow down the pool of suspects," I said.

"That sounds like a mixed metaphor but carry on," Micah said.

"You mentioned the problem of listing every racist in Worthing. Of course we can't do that but what we can do is list the active white supremacists as opposed to the common-or-garden racists. To be precise, the anti-racists of *Searchlight* probably can. They are very good at keeping track of the reptiles. I emailed them. They are sending over a list."

"It isn't just Worthing though," Micah said.

"I asked for Worthing and District."

Micah nodded and we started the house-to-house. I am never sure whether to bring Barker on these jaunts. He is a good ice-breaker but some people find a large Alsatian not to their taste. We compromised by taking it in turns to look after Barker while the other asked the questions.

"We are friends of Mr Moyes, we are investigating his death."

"The paper said it was natural causes – an accidental overdose of something or other."

"We don't think someone accidentally buried a doll with a stake through the heart in his garden."

"No that does stretch the credibility a bit, I quite understand but I don't see how I can help."

"Have you seen any strangers hanging around?"

"You're the first strangers I've seen in this street, apart from the police of course."

"Have you seen any cars that don't belong here?"

"Now you mention it, there was a white car I didn't recognise. It was quite late at night, a couple of days before Mr Moyes died. I don't take a note of registration numbers of course and I am not an expert on types of car."

"Did it seem a large car?"

"Not particularly, no but as I say I am no expert."

"If I give you a card, can you email or ring with any information you remember. It could be important."

"Certainly, Mr er McLairy. I wish I could be more help."

"Your information could be very useful. Anything else you can think of could also help us to build up a picture."

The weather was fine and the people seemed quite hospitable. We were offered several cups of tea and one slice of seed cake which was very nice. Some of the neighbours spotted Barker and invited him in so they could fuss and feed him. I think he put on several pounds during the course of the investigation.

We focussed on the white car and it turned out that three of the neighbours had noticed it. It was as unusual for a strange car to be in the road as for a doll with a stake through the heart to appear in a garden.

We got a partial number plate for a strange reason.

"I don't remember the number but the three letters were Golf November Uniform," they checked that Micah had written it down correctly and added, "Gnu, like the animal. That's why I remember it."

In itself this was not that useful. A thousand cars have those three letters in the numberplate. However, we had all the data *Searchlight* could provide if only we could find out there was a connection.

Micah could access the Police National Computer and within a day she had the registration numbers of all the fascist cars in Worthing and its environs. There was a problem. None of them had GNU on their registration plates.

It seemed that we had hit a brick wall. The next piece of information seemed unhelpful too.

I got a phone call from Sergeant Joanne Thallman.

"You have been looking for a white car with a number plate which includes the letters G, N and U."

"Yes."

"We have one."

"OK."

"You're not going to like it."

"Go ahead," I said.

"Yolanda Moughan owns a white BMW with a number which includes GNU."

"And you're sure?"

There was a silence which eloquently answered that.

So we needed to talk to Yolanda Moughan again. No tea this time.

"Don't bring that dirty animal in here."

Anyone who dislikes Barker is automatically suspect but I carried on while Micah took him for a short walk. I don't think Yolanda will be on Micah's Christmas Card list any time soon.

"It's about your car. Has it been stolen?"

"It's in the garage. Do you want to look?"

"I will have a look but did it go missing any time around the 25th?"

"No."

"Is it always kept in the garage?"

"No I had a little declutter of the garage last week because I didn't want it on the road. Vandalism you know."

"So it could have been stolen and returned?"

"What is all this in aid of, Mr McLairy?"

"A white car with GNU in the registration number was seen in the vicinity of Mr Moyes' house."

"Are you still going on about that doll? I thought you had better things to do."

"We think it's important."

"Well the car could have been stolen and returned but as far as I know it wasn't. Now do you want to look at the car or not?"

"It might be helpful."

She almost threw the car and garage keys at me.

"If you want to waste your time, be my guest."

I wore gloves in case there were fingerprints. If it had been stolen the thief probably wore gloves too. There were no prints on the doll for example. I examined the car but I could see nothing amiss.

I rang Sergeant Thallman.

"Joanne, I wonder if you could..."

"fingerprint Ms Moughan's car? I did that this morning. The only prints were hers. I think I might have put her back up."

"I can confirm that but thanks for the information. Are you tending towards the Voodoo theory now?"

"Unless you can come up with something else, yes. I don't want to believe it, Craig."

Joanne and her partner Janet came round for Dijon chicken that evening. We scrupulously avoided talking about the case but it was apparent that everyone around the table was struggling to keep off the topic. After dinner we succumbed.

"I think the prime projection," Joanne grinned, "I mean the most likely case is that one or some of the fascists on your list was aiming to discredit Voodoo and kill off an opponent all in one go. Using Yolanda's car was clever but there was no certainty that it would be spotted. So that thought wasn't followed through very carefully."

"There isn't enough evidence to charge Yolanda and I for one am pleased about that. Old Ben Tillotson takes a different view. He agrees about the lack of evidence, just not about Yolanda. Whoever stole the car left no fingerprints as you know. There are by the way a dozen cars with the letters GNU and half of them are white. A clever lawyer could make use of that."

"The overdose of cocaine could have been administered while Mr Moyes was asleep. By the time he woke it would be too late to do anything about it and he would be in no fit state to resist." Janet had been thinking about the case too.

"I can't tell you anything about Stubbins aka Byron Marcel. However he might have had a credible threat from a white supremacist."

"Did this fascist have a name that sounded foreign?" Micah asked innocently.

"You might think that, I couldn't possibly comment." Joanne was smiling.

Micah then said, "I've got an idea." She explained her idea and Joanne was all for trying it out immediately.

So it was in the middle of the night that she and a few hand-picked colleagues (we had to keep a discreet distance) knocked on the door of Mr Ernest Von Galt. She later reported to us that he had an impeccable upper-class English accent and he was not pleased to have his premises searched.

Either there was no cocaine on the premises or he had concealed it very well. That did not matter. The real target was his mobile phone.

"Is this your phone?"

"Yes. I will want a receipt for it."

Joanne slipped it into a plastic bag. She couldn't resist a beaming smile which Mr Von Galt did not like the look of at all.

As technical experts we were not allowed in on the interview at the station. We did ask.

It was the next day that Joanne and Janet met up with us in the Park View.

"White supremacists are a threat to public order and they sometimes, and this is one of those times, pose a terrorist threat. In those circumstances the full weight of the anti-terror legislation can be used against them," Joanne began.

Micah looked as though she had something to say but she was more interested in letting Joanne get on with the story.

"The most important thing about them is that they are not very bright. Any smart terrorist would have made sure their mobile phone was elsewhere or at the very least turned off. Von Galt very carefully made sure he left no fingerprints. However he knew nothing about Voodoo so his first mistake was to believe the flim flam about Voodoo dolls. As Yolanda rightly says, they are a myth."

"The doll did not bring about Mr Moyes' death. That was a massive dose of cocaine. Again Von Galt had the wit to make sure no cocaine was found at his home."

"What he also did was to have his mobile phone with him the whole time. The records of his service provider, which the anti-terror legislation allows us to access, placed him at the scene of the car theft and at Mr Moyes' address."

"Then his second big mistake. He was too arrogant to call a solicitor. So when we presented him with the evidence piece by piece, he was the one who went to pieces. He went into a rant about West Indians (Yolanda was born in the UK by the way) and the 'race traitors' who campaign against racism."

Janet took over, "I took down his statement and he was formally charged with the murder of Zacariah Arnold Moyes at 4 am this morning. I haven't had much sleep but I wanted you to know. It was Micah's idea, after all."

"And if you get any more ideas, you can help the police with their inquiries. It's my round I think." Joanne concluded.

# A Deed Without a Name

"Six months ago we had a case involving a poppet with a stake through the heart and now you want us to investigate witches flying around on broomsticks?"

Detective Sergeant Joanne Thallman and her partner Detective Constable Janet Small dropped in on one of our business meetings in the Brunswick and Thorn to make this unusual request.

To her credit, Joanne looked a bit embarrassed.

"There are no broomsticks involved," Micah liked to stick to the facts.

"Witches, though," I said, "in the twenty-first century?"

Micah produced her spiral-bound notebook from somewhere, I think she uses magic.

Joanne dictated from memory

- Grace Palmer IC1 female 56, dresses very smart no previous.

- Sherry Palmer IC1 female 54 sister of Grace, dresses Oxfam but smart no previous.

- Charity Arnold IC1 female twenties dresses M and S no previous.

- Three core members but various hangers-on

- Abel Wilks male IC1 52, no previous."

"No information about his clothes?" Micah asked.

Joanne smiled,

"He dresses like a man but I've never seen him myself. The other is one Felicity Newell IC1 female 60 who has got previous but it is for parking offences in the 1970s. Also she hasn't attended for some time."

"They tried meeting in a room at St Paul's Community Centre. What was strange about it was that they put a notice on the door, 'Poetry Group Do not disturb." Rather than 'Poetry Group, please come and join us.' A member of staff knocked on the door to ask what they were doing because there were complaints from other users. The answer he got through the door was 'A deed without a name'."

"Macbeth," said Micah, "but I won't list him as a suspect. Not yet."

"What were they doing?" I asked.

"Other users could hear chanting," Joanne said, "the upshot was that they were banned from St Paul's. We wouldn't have been interested but the member of staff who banned them, Iso Cousins, found a dead dog on his doorstep. No witnesses could be found. The dog seemed to be a stray which had had its throat cut and been drained of blood."

"That wasn't the end of it. Iso had a nasty road accident. Apparently a mobility scooter collided with his leg, it seemed accidental, and he wound up in the stream of traffic in Chapel Street and received multiple injuries. The mobility scooter just carried on as if nothing had happened. Nobody could identify the driver and of course there was no number plate."

"This seems to be the kind of thing we would investigate," Constable Janet Small explained, "but we were told in no uncertain terms to leave it and there is a reason."

"About five years ago, a child told his teacher that this coven (a coven of three not thirteen) had made him eat a cat. The matter was referred to social services and ended up in court. Their lawyer got the lad to confess it was a chocolate cat and the case collapsed. The press decided headlines about a 'Witch Hunt' were appropriate. So without very good evidence, there is nothing we can do about this coven."

They both looked at us. I took the opportunity to refill our glasses with the Brunswick and Thorn's Merlot.

"So is there something we can do?" Micah asked sweetly.

"We think you could infiltrate the group but it might be dangerous," Joanne suggested.

"I doubt if they go around putting cards in newsagents' windows," I said.

"Funny you should say that," Joanne smiled and produced a card.

"WORTHING WICCA

ANCIENT WISDOM

ANCIENT REMEDIES

INTERESTED?"

And there was a mobile phone number.

"This isn't the number for Satan?" Micah asked.

"No, they tell me his is 666,"

Micah and I were cautious about this job. We had one paying job on hand, the toilet case (don't ask) but it easily left us enough time for an evening of Satanism per fortnight. I kept track of Micah's location using her phone and she transmitted all her conversation in real time despite the phenomenal drain on the battery.

"You knock on the door and say, 'What is it you do?' OK? Then we let you in."

"What is it you do?"

"A deed without a name."

Cue laughter. I will avoid the term cackling but it sounded like it. We decided that either the staff at St Paul's community centre had accidentally hit on a password or the coven of three had decided it was such a hoot they couldn't resist incorporating it in their ritual.

Micah described the evening as more like a Women's Institute gathering than anything else. How she knows when she has never been a member of the WI is one of life's little mysteries.

There were minutes of the previous meeting, matters arising, points of order, correspondence. I found myself dozing off but I was fully awake when the singing began.

I don't think Grace, Sherry or Charity would ever be much of an ornament to a choir. Micah has a lovely singing voice but she was a little hesitant because the songs were unfamiliar. One was a version of the Paternoster set to music and meticulously reversed. The others sounded like folk songs but they were not commonplace ones. To listen to these refined voices joining in quite bawdy lyrics – some of them in Latin – was an experience.

As a kind of closing prayer, one of the voices said, "Do what thou wilt shall be the whole of the law." Micah identified it as the voice of Grace Palmer.

It was Grace who had a little talk with Micah after the meeting.

"You are having trouble with your elbow joint."

"Yes does it show?"

"It's all right, dear, I just noticed. Wait here a minute."

There was a pause.

"If you rub it with this and say these words, 'lex quae potest facere quod libet' that's a rough translation of the prayer into Latin. Satan understands Latin better than English you know."

Micah immediately enlisted the support of our daughter Dorothy. We had her round for a meal. Spaghetti carbonara and a couple of bottles of Casillero del Diablo Cabernet Sauvignon got Dorothy asking, "And what can I do for you?"

Micah handed over the potion. Dorothy took a sniff cautiously and looked at it with distaste.

"Is this a case you two are working on?"

"Yes?"

"Has anybody been poisoned with this?"

"It is for external application together with a magic spell," Micah said.

"Look, if you don't want to tell me..."

"I am telling you. I will not use it but it would be interesting to know what it contains."

"OK, give me a week," our long-suffering daughter conceded.

In the meantime, Micah adopted a more conventional Ibuprofen gel for her elbow. She didn't mutter any spells over it.

Dorothy emailed within three days. "The gunk is for external application only. It will do neither good nor harm. If taken internally the victim should take steps to get it back up again ASAP. Contents include turmeric, calendula, black cumin oil, liquorice and the surprise ingredient urtica dioica which is the common stinging nettle."

All this information was passed on to Janet Thallman. For the next two meetings it was more of the same and there was an unspoken feeling that we would get nothing out of Micah's infiltration of the wee coven. We were wrong.

The next meeting, we realised later, coincided with the full moon. It was rather different.

"Micah, do you have a five pound note?" asked Charity.

A minute later, Charity said,

"Treasurer's report. Micah just gave me five pounds."

The laughter seemed disproportionate.

Grace said, "This is Abel, Micah, he always comes to these special meetings, don't you, Abel?"

Micah later voiced an apprehension that she would have to kiss the old goat in some way but thankfully that didn't happen.

"Tea."

It wasn't a polite inquiry but an instruction from the arch-witch Grace. Micah revealed that she took one sip of it and then left it. When the attention of the others was distracted she looked around for a potted plant but there was none. As an improvisation she poured it into her bag regardless of the mess it would make of everything. The others, she thought, did not notice. She can be sly when she wants to.

There was an uninhibited discussion about "Do what thou wilt" and to say these people were Thatcher's children would be an underestimate. They all revelled in acts of selfishness in which they had overcome their "cowardly consciences" and this culminated in the two Palmer sisters, saying the following:

Grace said, "Our mother just seemed to get old and frail very fast and we had to wait on her hand, foot and finger. We told the doctor that she just wouldn't eat."

Sherry added, "That was because we didn't give the old bat any food."

The two sisters' laughter was positively Mephistophelian. The others, including Micah, joined in.

Grace continued, "The thing we had to make sure..."

However Charity cut this discussion short by beginning to sing. Her delivery was a bit shaky. The others joined in but the singing became incoherent quite rapidly.

Abel said, "Right."

Over the phone I could not tell what was right but Micah tells me they all stood up and faced one direction, possibly East.

I heard the next bit. It was a scream, a horrific scream. Micah joined in for form's sake and Abel joined in in a lower key.

By now I was in the car with Barker. I thought this had gone on long enough. I parked in the road next to the coven HQ but I stayed where I was. Micah had anticipated my response and made the occasional quiet comment to let me know she was OK.

"Look down," Charity ordered, "Look, the lights of Worthing, can you see?"

They all made noises of assent and throughout their flight of fancy Charity kept up a running commentary.

"There's the Lido, there's the pier. Can you see what that couple are doing in that flat over there?"

Micah admitted that she had a momentary thought about people getting net curtains because by then she was caught up in the fantasy.

"Feel the night breeze. Look at those ordinary people, the swarming freight of gregarious life. How great to soar above them, feel the power of Satan. We are powerful, we can do anything..." and so forth.

By common consent they came back down to earth. The meeting concluded with the usual prayer. Abel made a clumsy overture towards Micah. In keeping with her role she responded in kind.

"But aren't you married?" said the old goat.

"Do what thou wilt," said Micah brightly, adding, "Will I see you in 28 days time?"

"We could meet earlier than that. You know, just go for a drink."

Micah made a date with the venerable Capra. As she left, I told her where the car was.

"Were you worried about me? How sweet," she said.

"Worried with reason I thought."

"There was something in that tea, that's for sure. I must see if Joanne can get it analysed. The collective hallucination was powerful or they are all perfect playactors. I think I will concentrate on the full moon meetings in future, become a social member of the coven like Abel."

"Ah yes, your friend with capricorn tendencies."

"He also had hercine tendencies. He smelt like an old goat as well when I got close to him," Micah laughed.

Then she was serious again.

"The beginning of the meeting was like the opposite of a confession. There is no contrition, they revel in wrongdoing, they boast. The boasts, you heard them, they were all minor except the Palmer sisters. We must see what Joanne can come up with on that score. Anything she can tell me about Abel might be useful. I think this is our best chance of finding out about the coven."

"Now, how about a nightcap to take away the taste of that tea?"

We settled on Laphroaig.

It was two days later that Joanne could get us any information, the examination of the contents of the handbag took that long.

"Micah, the lab report suggests you were right about the tea. It picked up all sorts of chemicals from your handbag contents but it contained a significant amount of Psilocybin which comes from Magic Mushrooms which grow all over Sussex. They are a so-called controlled drug but their prevalence makes them very difficult to control. We could raid the coven on the next full moon and catch them using an illegal substance but we are more interested in more serious criminal matters so we'll keep that on the back burner for now."

"The death of Mrs Palmer was attributed to a heart attack. It was a Doctor Winter, oh stop laughing, this is serious. She did have signs of malnutrition. Her daughters said at the time they were making efforts to get her to eat more."

"The admission you heard was made under the influence of drugs and it was recorded illegally. It is informative but not evidence. You know all this."

"I said Abel Wilks had no previous and that is strictly true. There have been no allegations proved against him. The witnesses all changed their stories or decided it wasn't him after all. I don't think he put a spell on them. Anything you can get out of him would be useful."

"Can you tell me anything about the allegations?"

"Of course I can do no such thing, Micah."

There was a pause.

"By the way, how old were you last birthday?"

Micah told her.

"Well you should be safe, you are roughly fifty years too old for Mr Wilks to take any interest."

"Oh I see."

"One last thing.."

And she told Micah one last thing.

The setting was a local pub. I'm not recommending it, it was Abel Wilks' choice and the carpet squelched underfoot. I was in one bar sampling their very average Merlot. Micah had arrived early. Abel was slightly deaf so I didn't need to use any equipment to eavesdrop. It would have been conspicuous. I was there in person with Barker because, despite Joanne's assurances, I was not happy about this meeting.

"I could tell you were coming," Micah said when Abel arrived, "by the pricking of my thumbs."

He seemed to take this as a compliment.

"What can I get you, my dear?" he asked.

Micah opted for the Merlot. It was probably safer than anything else on offer. She watched the glass all the way from the bar. Abel was probably quite capable of adding something untoward to a woman's drink.

"Cheers."

"I really enjoyed that meeting," Micah began.

"It's called a Sabat," he said inaccurately. Micah decided not to question his Satanic knowledge.

"That Sabat. It was exciting and different. I've never experienced anything like it in my life! ."

"Really?"

"It's as if the four of you put a spell on me."

Abel laughed at that.

"Between you and me," he whispered, he didn't realise his whisper was audible in the next bar, possibly in the next street, "some of the magic spells aren't what they seem. Oh, we curse people, curse them good and proper with all the right rituals. I see to that. But after that, well, let's just say the Devil helps those who help themselves."

"Years ago a silly little girl thought she could get the better of me. I went to the coven and we held a ritual to curse her if she ever gave evidence against me.

"The thing is, I wanted to make assurance doubly sure as Shakespeare would have done. I got her alone. I told her I might go to prison so she would be safe from me but I knew people, nasty people. And I suggested they might take it into their heads to set her house on fire and burn her family to death. That would have been sad, wouldn't it?"

"The long and short of it was that she never gave evidence against me. Nobody betrays me, Micah, remember that. Can I get you another?"

"Well, I have to get back to give the dog a walk but maybe just one more."

This time the incompetent goat actually turned his back on Micah while he was bringing the drink to the table. His back was turned so long that she didn't need to see him putting the rohypnol substitute into the glass.

Micah played with him, picking up the glass as if to drink then putting it down to speak. If you have ever seen a dog following every mouthful of food to your mouth with his eyes you can imagine what an amusing sight our old goat made for Micah.

"And you see, the Palmer sisters didn't just rely on the curse we put on their old mother either did they? Do drink up, dear. No, they just didn't feed her. The body was cremated so nothing has been proved. Now just drink that up like a good girl and I'll tell you something else about the ... oh shit!"

The last remark was prompted by Micah accidentally knocking her glass and sending the mediocre Merlot all over his shirt.

"Oh look, Abel, I am sorry is there anything I can..." she dabbed at his shirt front with her handkerchief.

"Stop it, you stupid...no sorry I didn't mean that, let me just get you another."

"My round," Micah said swiftly and bought the drinks before he could.

"Quite recently," he continued, "a nasty piece of work at St Paul's banned us from meeting there. It's not as if it was a church. It's just a community centre. Well he met with a nasty accident. Look it up in the local paper if you don't believe me. It does not pay to get on the wrong side of us, Micah. Though I am sure you wouldn't dream of doing that, would you dear?"

"Yes I bloody would," said Micah but she said that to me after her date from Hell was over and done with.

We had mushroom with crème fraîche and potatoes for dinner and Joanne and Janet joined us. The dinner was late because they had a crisis at work.

"Iso Cousins, the St Paul's employee with the complex injuries was transferred to a specialist unit in Croydon," said Janet, "the poor blighter was DOA."

She let that sink in.

"So it is a murder case," I like stating the obvious.

"Yes. However the information has not been shared with the media as yet."

"That's interesting," said Micah.

"Have you got an idea?"

And she had.

The Worthing Herald website had the following,

"Mr Iso Cousins, the St Paul's employee who was a victim of a hit and run involving a mobility scooter, is sufficiently recovered to be questioned by police in the near future. Inspector Tillotson of the Worthing Constabulary said that he was confident that the witness would be able to positively identify his assailant."

DC Janet Small was back in uniform for her task of guarding the room in which Mr Cousins was supposedly being treated. She noticed the man wearing a cleaning company uniform and mopping the floor in the main ward and paid him no attention. Just a cleaner.

She quite happily let him into the room to clean. When he saw the figure in the bed in the dim blue light, he expertly disabled the life support system and the alarm which would sound if life support were switched off.

He hadn't noticed as Janet had followed him into the ward. The first he knew about it was when she pushed him to the ground and put the cuffs on him, none too gently. Still keeping him down by the simple device of sitting on him she said,

"Mr Abel Wilks I am arresting you for the attempted murder of ... well ... a crash test dummy. And for the murder of Mr Iso Cousins."

At the interview they were able to produce the witness statement which identified the driver of the mobility scooter as a male.

Then they produced the report of the search of his home, which showed the mobility scooter with damage consistent with the assault on Mr Cousins.

Then they produced his diary which they had also seized.

"For the benefit of the tape, the suspect is smiling."

"Well that will do you a fat lot of good."

"Do you admit this is your diary?"

"Of course. Would you care to read me a bit of it."

Joanne read out a series of meaningless groups of letters. Mr Wilks actually laughed and that was caught on tape.

Joanne translated, "I got a real thrill from that elegant revenge on the St Paul's busybody. I am only sorry I couldn't hang about to see him being mangled by the passing traffic in Chapel Street."

"For the benefit of the tape, Mr Wilks is catching flies with his mouth."

"Mr Wilks, this diary has been very useful to us in a number of ongoing investigations. Everything from the death of Mrs Palmer to the supply of dangerous drugs. You have incriminated your fellow practitioners just like in any witch hunt. It will also enable us to re-open the case on which you were acquitted because it is new evidence."

"But.."

"But me no buts. It is all here in black and white. By the way, Micah McLairy wanted to inform you that she decyphered what she called your pathetic encryption in this diary."

"That bitch. I'll strangle her with my bare hands."

"That will not sound good in court, Mr Wilks."

"No comment."

# Killed by a corpse

"There was something wrong about the death of Alex Michael. Inspector Tillotson was all set to sign it off as suicide but he has given me, given us, a couple of days to review the evidence." Sergeant Joanne Thallman had casually dropped in to one of our business meetings in the John Selden to share this.

"Alex Michael's body was found in a locked room, his landlady called the fire brigade to break the door down. He had shot himself. The gun was a Smith & Wesson M&P which he owned legally and used at a gun club. It was normally kept at the club but members sometimes take them away despite the rules. Mr Michael had put the gun in his mouth. It is the most efficient way to commit suicide. I doubt if it tastes very nice but that is not a problem for long. One odd thing was that the gun was in his left hand but Mr Michael was one of those rare individuals who are genuinely ambidextrous."

"Was there a note?"

"60 percent of male suicides do not leave a note but Mr Michael did leave a verbal message with his doctor, Dr Steven Johnstone. He was treating Mr Michael for depression and it seems that threats to kill himself were fairly routine so the doc didn't pay any special attention to it."

"I interviewed him and he certainly seems to regret it now. If he is an average GP, he has about a thousand patients but he seemed to take this personally."

"Mr Michael had been a teacher of semiotics. However he lost his job in a reorganisation three years back and has been struggling to find a permanent job ever since. It was during this period that his depression deteriorated as far as Dr Johnstone was aware."

Joanne then showed us a sketch plan and some photos of the room. One thing struck us immediately. The lock was a mortice deadlock with a keyhole inside and outside. I looked at Micah and she smiled.

"Did anyone hear the gun shot?" I asked.

Joanne shook her head, "Mr Michael lived alone since he parted company with his girlfriend, Pet Penrose (Micah duly noted this down as well as Ms Penrose's address). The landlady was shopping. The room below Mr Michael's was empty and the room next to it was the room of Mr Potting who is deaf. We knocked on his door for a while before we got any response and the landlady, Mrs Grove, confirmed that Mr Potting wasn't winding us up."

"We will interview him anyway, background on the victim," I said.

"So, you think he was a victim?"

"I have an open mind, Joanne, but 'victim' will do until we know otherwise."

Micah nodded.

"I can arrange for you to have access to the room tomorrow. I know you still have your police technical adviser ID so there should not be a problem."

The next day, the sunny weather broke and a more English drizzle took its place.

Micah took the lead with the interview with Mr Potting. We found out his name was Frank but very little else. He was in his early sixties and had retired from the railways where deafness hadn't prevented him from working. He had always been deaf.

Micah is an expert in sign language. So was Mr Potting. It was a pity they both used different systems of sign language. A semiologist like the late Mr Michael would have found it amusing. In the end we wrote each other notes.

No, Mr Potting didn't know his neighbour very well. He (Mr Potting) kept himself to himself. He never had to complain about the noise. For Mr Potting this was the best of jokes.

He made us tea. We left him a business card. He had a smartphone and could easily text us if anything occurred to him.

We examined the room. Every bloodstain (and a bullet through the top of the head leaves a fair few) was marked and numbered. There was an array of works of fiction and a number of books on semiotics, postmodernism and linguistics. I pointed out Dorothy Rowe's classic *Depression, the way out of your prison* which seemed to have been read more than once.

"We must ask the police about one thing which seems to be missing," Micah said.

"The absence of medication?"

Micah made a noise like 'hm' and got to work downloading the files from the computer onto a memory stick.

When we got home she reviewed it on her laptop.

She was silent for a while but then she said, "I hope to God you haven't got anything like this on your computer, Craig."

I looked over her shoulder at the rather steamy email exchanges between Alex and Pet.

"I'll delete it," I promised.

"You'd better," said Micah and resumed her reading.

The Police Technical Adviser ID could open a lot of doors. Barker was usually quite good at getting interviewees at their ease. However Ms Penrose did not like dogs. She went down in my estimation immediately.

However, I took Barker for a walk while Micah conducted the interview. Micah has obtained a tiny recharger for her phone and it sits with the phone in her handbag. So while I was walking Barker I could use an earphone to listen in to the conversation which Micah was also recording.

Apparently, the conversation was "end to end encrypted" whatever that means which had the result that nobody else could listen in to it. Micah's bad habits have taught her to be cautious of the phone-hacking of others.

I should mention that Pet Penrose had got the idea that Micah was an inspector because that was a common rank among TV detectives.

"No, inspector, you've got it all wrong. It is true that Alex and I had parted company but we never actually lived together. Sometimes I went to his and sometimes he came here. And sometimes he would come round for a meal as a friend. In fact the last time was, let me look at the calendar, the 5th of July. We had lamb. It was delicious."

If Micah reacted to the date, Pet didn't apparently notice.

"Alex and I have broken up before and somehow we always got together again. Sometimes he could talk Semiotics for a solid hour and scarcely notice I was there and sometimes he was dysphoric – which means a miserable old git in common English."

"But there was never anybody else. He smiled at other women and occasionally licked his lips. I had to tell him about that. However, he seemed sort-of lost without me and he could be good fun sometimes when he wasn't in one of his dark moods. I refuse to believe that he killed himself point blank – if that's the right thing to say given there was a gun involved. Even if he did, it was not over me. We were still friends. We had been more than friends. I miss him. I miss him more than I can say."

"I am sorry you had to send your dog away. I don't dislike dogs but I am allergic to them. If there is anything else I can do to help, you will let me know?"

"There is just one thing. Alex told his doctor that he was suicidal. How do you explain that?"

"Alex didn't have a doctor. He never took any medication. That was one of his problems, I think. He had a fear of anti-depressants. He had a student once who was addicted to ADs so he wouldn't touch them."

"Doctor Steven Johnstone told us..."

"I beg your pardon."

"Doctor Steven Johnstone"

Pet gave a laugh that had very little humour in it.

"Alex's mother died two years ago. Alex always said that Doctor Steven bloody Johnstone had killed her."

"How do you mean?"

"Alex talked about this a lot. She had cancer. If the incompetent swine had been any use she would have been diagnosed sooner and she would still be alive. Alex dwelt on it. You see if he did have a doctor it would have been one of those homosexuals."

"Homeopaths?"

"Yes one of those. But I don't think he had a doctor at all."

The phrase "Can I help you?" can be said in such a way that it is intimidating and suggests you are an intruder who has no business to be there. That was how the landlady, Mrs Holly Grove, greeted us.

"We are looking into the background of the unfortunate death of Mr Michael."

"Suicide. It was suicide, not an 'unfortunate death'. All deaths are unfortunate for somebody Mr (she read my badge) McLairy. I don't know as how I can help very much. I leave my guests to get on with their own lives, I am not the nosy kind of landlady. They do what they like so long as they don't make a lot of noise and they pay their rent on the dot. I am very particular about that."

"Did he seem gloomy to you?"

"You mean about the time of his 'unfortunate death'? Well he were no more gloomy than normal. That Miss Penrose now, nice polite young lady, she said he was dysphoric and that sent me scurrying to the dictionary. If he had mood swings they were long-lasting and gloomy. He cheered up with her of course but then she'd cheer anybody up."

"We knew it were suicide on account of the door being locked *on the inside* you see."

We spent an interesting twenty minutes in which I showed her how to lock and unlock a door from the outside when there is a key in the lock. It required a metal tube into which an average key shaft fits with a slot for the bit (technical term for the operative part of a key). I just happen to have one. I don't know that she trusted me any more after that.

"Well that will be useful if the same thing ever happens again. God forbid!" was her comment.

Micah made a neat list of the suspects.

- Dr Steven Johnstone
- Pet Penrose

- Frank Potting
- Holly Grove
- Alex Michael

"So far," she said, "only Alex Michael had a motive. However, there is an erased file on his laptop which raises a few questions. It is a letter setting out his views on his mother's death. They do not provide proof positive of Dr Johnstone's negligence but they are enough for the BMA to want to investigate further."

"The question is: who erased the file?"

"When was it erased?"

"On the very night of his suicide."

That evening we were in the John Selden playing our favourite game of plotting the course of the galaxy for the next thousand years. It's a version of 'putting the world to rights' but on a grand scale.

We were brought down to earth by a visit from Inspector Ben Tillotson.

"You can buy me a drink. I've got some very interesting information for you. Here."

He handed over a number of stills from the CCTV in the street adjacent to the one in which Alex Michael died. The photos suggested it probably was not a suicide. In any case someone had to explain their presence.

"There's another thing," said Micah. "Alex Michael had a friendly dinner with Pet Penrose at exactly the same time as he was making his verbal statement to Doctor Johnstone. He can't be in two places at once."

Old Ben nodded with satisfaction.

"My sergeant is putting a few questions to the good doctor as we speak. Could you just text her that little gem, Micah?"

"Already passed it on."

Ben's smile grew wider but as usual his pockets remained very deep and his arms very short.

Ben was not happy the next time we saw him.

"The problem is," he said, "doctors have access to a hundred ways of killing themselves. We didn't have enough evidence to remand him in custody. Once we had checked his alibi of visiting a patient in that road we would have done."

"In the good old days we would have said he'd cheated the hangman."

"This particular suicide did leave a note. It's two pages of doctorly scrawl so I will summarise it. He has, or rather had, a horror of prison, after all it is supposed to be a deterrent. He knew that Mr Michael would go on digging until he found out the truth about his mother and the doctor could not let that happen."

"Mr Michael was technically his patient, the whole family were his patients, but Mr Michael had never visited the doctor."

"The landlady was a patient and he recognised her in Tesco's. He didn't know the neighbour was deaf so he took a ridiculous chance. He went to Mr Michael to talk the whole thing over man to man. Mr Michael was either cleaning his gun or admiring it, in any case he left it on the table. The murder was quick and efficient. A pity the doc wasn't more so with his patients."

"You might say Alex Michael killed him from beyond the grave," I said.

"A bit fanciful, Craig."

Printed in Great
Britain
by Amazon